Ann Was Sorry To Find Herself Back At Her Own Front Gate.

She didn't want to go back into her house. Not tonight. Tonight, she wanted to feel the warmth of Niall's hand, the big, solid strength of his body. And when he let go of her hand to unlatch the gate, she wanted to protest like a disappointed child, to cry out loud, No! Not yet, not yet!

She was shaking inside, hot and cold at the same time. She told herself, Annie, don't be a fool! He's a stranger. He doesn't belong here. In a few days, he'll be gone, and in another week, he won't remember your name!

She knew it was true, but something in her cried like that stubborn, disappointed child, I don't care, I don't care! And it took every bit of willpower she had to turn away from him and push open the door.

Dear Reader:

Happy summertime reading from everyone here! July is an extra-special month, because Nora Roberts—at long last—has written a much-anticipated Silhouette Desire. It's called *A Man for Amanda* and it's part of her terrific series, THE CALHOUN WOMEN. Look for the distinctive portrait of Amanda Calhoun on the cover.

And also look for the portrait of July's *Man of the Month,* Niall Rankin, on the cover of Kathleen Creighton's *In From the Cold*. Ms. Creighton has written a number of books for Silhouette Intimate Moments. Please *don't* miss this story; I know you'll love it!

There is something for everyone this month—sensuous, emotional romances written just for *you!* July is completed with other must-reads from the talented pens of your *very* favorites: Helen R. Myers, Barbara Boswell, Joan Johnston and Linda Turner. So enjoy, enjoy....

All the best,

Lucia Macro
Senior Editor

KATHLEEN CREIGHTON

IN FROM THE COLD

SILHOUETTE *Desire*®

Published by Silhouette Books New York

America's Publisher of Contemporary Romance

SILHOUETTE BOOKS
300 East 42nd St., New York, N.Y. 10017

IN FROM THE COLD

ISBN: 0-373-05654-0

First Silhouette Books printing July 1991

Books by Kathleen Creighton

Silhouette Intimate Moments

Demon Lover #84
Double Dealings #157
Gypsy Dancer #196
In Defense of Love #216
Rogue's Valley #240
Tiger Dawn #289
Love and Other Surprises #322

Silhouette Desire

The Heart Mender #584
In From the Cold #654

KATHLEEN CREIGHTON

has roots deep in the California soil and still lives in the valley where her mother and grandmother were born. As a child, she enjoyed listening to old timers' tales, and her fascination with the past only deepened as she grew older. Today, she says she is interested in everything—art, music, gardening, zoology, anthropology and history, but people are at the top of her list. She also has a lifelong passion for writing, and recently began to combine her two loves into romance novels.

One

Rankin was tired. Tired of looking at the blacktop pavement, its headlighted wedge a constant he couldn't escape, like a ghost image burned in his retinas. Tired of the thrumming of tires, of engine sounds and wind and air-conditioning, the insidious pressure in his ears that stayed with him even long after he'd stopped for the night. Tired of the crackling of the country music stations that faded in and out on the car's stereo. Tired of the *smell,* that unmistakable rental car smell of air freshener over old tobacco.

He could have stopped in any one of the small towns he'd passed through that day, towns that lined the highway between Reno and L.A., alike as beads on a chain, seeming to have no other reason for existence except as oases for tired travelers like himself. He'd passed one only five or ten miles back, in fact, and as he'd slowed for the blinking yellow caution light at the main intersection, he'd thought hard about pulling into one of the neon-lighted motels. In the middle of a springtime week like this, with the snow melting in the High Sierra ski resorts, there were few No Vacancy signs.

But he was tired of motel rooms, too. And truck-stop coffee. He longed for a good cup of tea—Darjeeling, preferably—and a bed that didn't feel like a mortuary slab. Both were waiting for him in L.A., along with the offer of a job that, if he decided to accept it, would effectively catapult him into a conventional house-in-the-suburbs existence for the first time in his life. And what irony it would be, he thought, if the infamous L.A. freeways managed to accomplish what almost twenty-five years on the frontlines of the Cold War had failed to do.

Highly unlikely. Rankin considered the prospect of his own demise with a thin, bitter smile. He had a healthy sense of self-preservation, and experience had taught him his own limits as well as how to push himself safely to their edge and no further. Which possibly explained why he was still alive when so many others weren't.

He frowned, stretched, squelched a fleeting desire for a cigarette, then rolled down his window an inch or two. The desert air was cold, and smelled of unfamiliar vegetation. After a moment he rolled the window up again. With a low mutter of annoyance he turned off the struggling country music station and punched in a tape instead, something called Bach's Greatest Hits he'd picked up in a car wash in Denver, for the hundredth time kicking himself for not remembering to bring along a supply from his own library of classics.

Not that he minded country music; in fact, he found the melodies themselves remarkably pleasing to the ears. It was the lyrics that got to him. They all seemed to have to do with homes and families, husbands and wives, sweethearts and lovers, belonging to someone, working things out. Either that or loneliness, heartache and betrayal. The first list Rankin had never known and so couldn't really identify with. The latter he knew entirely too well.

Which, he readily admitted, was no one's fault but his own. He'd chosen his course in life. And for the most part had never regretted those choices. For the most part...

And that included the choice that had put him where he was at the moment, driving from one coast to the other in a rented car instead of taking the usual course—a nonstop flight on a jumbo jet.

The job offer in L.A. had come as a surprise, and from an unexpected source. He'd met millionaire industrialist Joseph Varga several years before, during a covert operation involving the rescue of a certain scientist from behind the Iron Curtain. As a result of that operation Varga had spent six months in an Eastern bloc prison. Rankin had been at least partly to blame for getting him into that prison, and wholly instrumental in getting him out. Because of that, and for other reasons Rankin didn't like to dwell on, he and Varga had become friends. The day the Berlin Wall came down, Varga had telephoned, half-jokingly suggesting that since Rankin would soon be out of a job in the National Security Agency, he ought to consider industrial espionage for a change. He'd further suggested Rankin come to L.A. for a visit and to check out the possibility of working for him. It was hard to say who had been more surprised when Rankin accepted—Joseph, or Rankin.

And as for driving, he'd told himself—and anyone else who'd asked—that he had a vacation due, and he wanted to see the country. That after all he'd been American for nearly half his forty-four years, and had never been west of the Alleghenies. And that was part of it. But the rest wasn't that simple. He couldn't explain it to himself, and didn't even try to explain it to others. He just knew that he was searching for something he couldn't put a name to. And he knew that whatever it was, as of right now, only a few hours from his destination, he still hadn't found it.

Tired. Oh yes, he was tired, in more ways than one. And no one to blame but himself. Rankin shook his head in wry self-reproach and began to tap his fingers on the steering wheel in time to the slow rhythm of "Jesu, Joy of Man's Desiring," hoping that would help keep him alert.

When he caught the movement in the periphery of his headlights, his first thought was that he was seeing things—a hallucination brought on by fatigue or highway hypnosis. His second thought was coyote!

His foot jerked reflexively toward the brake pedal. Then stomped it hard as he identified *two* dark shapes, one of them almost certainly human. He was past them in an instant, but the image of a pale face and entreating eyes remained indelibly stamped on his retinas.

He brought the rental car to a crunching stop on the shoulder, swearing under his breath. *"Damn bloody fool kid."*

He sat grimly, watching his rearview mirror like a video monitor as the hitchhiker jogged toward him along the pavement's edge, a large, black dog shambling behind. Then the passenger door opened, illuminating a very young, somewhat flushed face and long wisps of light brown hair beneath the bill of a baseball cap.

Damned stupid, foolish little girl . . .

The minute she opened the door, Sunny had a feeling she might be in big trouble. She knew hitchhiking was dangerous—everybody knew that, plus she'd seen that movie, that awful one about the crazy guy who kept killing everybody—but she'd figured the odds were in her favor. What were the chances she'd get picked up by a rapist or an ax-murderer, especially way out here on the desert? Most of that stuff happened in big cities, anyway. And besides, she had Sarge.

So how come the minute she got a good look at the guy who'd stopped to give her a ride, she felt a cold, sick feeling in her middle?

Since her head was already half inside the car she opened her mouth to say something. Just something basic like, "Hi," or "Thanks, mister." But nothing came out. It felt as if something were stuck in her throat.

The man just sat there looking at her. She'd intended to ask him how far he was going—she was hoping for L.A. Now she started to back away instead. But right then Sarge plunked himself down on her foot, just as if he'd made up his own mind about the situation.

"Well, get in," the man said, pleasantly enough.

His face was pleasant, too, and he was nicely dressed, a lot nicer than most of the guys she knew. He had on a light-colored sweater that looked soft and expensive, and his pants weren't jeans. He looked elegant, like somebody in a magazine ad. She didn't know exactly what it was about him that frightened her, but something did.

She shook her head and managed to say, "Um...no thanks, mister. I think I'll just—"

A cool, quiet voice interrupted. "I was under the impression that you were trying to hitch a ride."

There was a little smile on his face, but his eyes weren't smiling, and Sunny decided then and there that it was his eyes that were scary. The way he looked at her made her feel like he could see inside her head, even the parts *she* couldn't bear to look at.

Plus the fact that he was so big. She *hated* tall people. People who were a lot bigger than she was made her nervous—which meant just about everyone. She hated being short. And fat. And it was very hard not to be fat when you were only five feet one. Just having *breasts* made you look fat. It was just one of the many things she blamed her mother for—both that and being five-one—and the really rotten part of it was her mother managed to have both of those things without looking the least bit fat. It wasn't fair.

"I changed my mind," she said to the man in the driver's seat, trying to be cool about it, trying to nudge Sarge off her foot without the man noticing what she was doing. She didn't think it would be a good idea to let him know that she was more or less trapped. "I, um, well see, I've got my dog with me, and he's pretty dirty, and you've got a really nice car, and I don't want to—"

"Get in the car," the man said, not smiling anymore.

The cold, sick feeling rose to Sunny's throat. No longer concerned with "cool," she shrank away, shaking her head rapidly.

The man's calm, reasonable voice followed her, mocking her wildly pounding heart. "Look, where do you think you're going to go? There's no one around for miles, and I can outrun you in two steps."

"I—I'll sic my dog on you," Sunny declared. Sarge grinned up at her, tongue lolling.

All the man did was make a soft sound, halfway between a snort and laughter, but this time when he ordered Sunny to get in the car, she found herself doing as she was told.

"Your dog, too," he said. But Sarge was way ahead of him. He was already crowding into the front seat, practically on top of her.

"Shut the door. And fasten your seatbelt." The man snapped orders at Sunny as he put the car in drive without even looking at her, just taking it for granted that she'd obey. She did, too. And because she hated taking orders almost more than anything, she began to feel a lot more angry than scared.

Sarge settled himself across Sunny's feet, groaned and laid his muzzle down on his paws. Sunny glared at him resentfully. Stupid old dog. Some protector he'd turned out to be. Didn't even care if it was an ax-murderer who'd picked them up, as long as he got a ride.

But for some reason she felt easier about the situation. She wondered if maybe Sarge knew something she didn't.

"May I ask where you think you're going?" the man inquired as he pulled out onto the highway. His tone was very polite—sarcastic, Sunny thought—and for the first time she noticed that he had a funny way of talking, some kind of accent. It made him seem even more like someone she'd read about in a magazine, or a character in a movie.

She glanced over at him and said, "L.A." When he just looked at her with one eyebrow a little higher than the other she improvised glibly, "To visit my aunt."

He made that soft noise again, and after a moment said conversationally, "Didn't anyone ever tell you that hitchhiking's dangerous?"

"Oh, I do it all the time," Sunny said, trying her best to sound plausible. "I take Sarge with me." At the sound of his name Sarge looked up, the tan thumbprints over his eyes twitching as he shifted them from Sunny to the man and back again.

The man looked down at Sarge and drawled, "Right." Then he flicked another glance at Sunny. "Perhaps a better question is, where are you from?"

Sunny stuck her chin in the air and rudely countered, "Where are *you* from?" By this time she was pretty sure the man wasn't going to rape or murder her and she was ticked off at him for scaring her to death. Besides, she really was curious. Not too many foreigners passed through Pinetree, California, which was where she'd lived all her life, and which she was sick to death of, and couldn't wait to get out of, even if it meant hitchhiking all the way to L.A. with a huge and vaguely menacing stranger.

The stranger lifted one eyebrow at her, as if he knew what she was thinking about him and found it mildly amusing. She shrugged defensively. "I noticed you have kind of an accent. So I wondered."

He murmured, "I do? That's funny, I didn't think I did." Sunny couldn't tell whether he was surprised or amused at that, but in any case, he didn't answer her question. Instead he made a U-turn, right in the middle of the highway.

"What are you doing?" gasped Sunny, grabbing for the door handle as a new fear clutched at her insides. "Where are you going?"

The man sounded thoughtful. "Hmm . . . Seems to me I remember a sheriff's station in that little town I passed through a while ago—what's it called?"

"Pinetree," said Sunny dismally as she settled back in her seat, folding her arms across her middle in a vain attempt to quiet the quivering there. A moment later, though, she was sitting bolt upright again—as far as she could with Sarge snoring on top of her sneakers. Her voice rose to a childish squeak. "Sheriff? Hey, wait a minute, you can't— I thought—you said you were going to L.A.!"

The man considered. "No, I don't believe I said where I was going. I asked where you were going."

"I want out," Sunny announced. "Stop this car right now."

"The way I see it," the man said, ignoring her order, "you've got two choices. You can tell me where you live and I'll take you there, or I'll leave you with the sheriff and let him figure out what to do with you. It's your choice. Either way. I personally don't care."

Yeah, why should you be any different, Sunny thought bleakly, and turned her face to the window. She watched the chamber of commerce's "Welcome to Pinetree" sign flash by on her right and then said in a muffled voice, "I live here, in Pinetree. On Sierra Avenue. Turn right at the light."

"That's better," the man murmured, smug in his victory. "Now, how about a name? I assume you have one."

"Yeah, it's Sunshine—as in 'ray of,'" Sunny said nastily, and turned back to the window. She decided that she hated the big man in the elegant clothes more than she'd ever hated anyone in her whole entire life, even Will Clemson. Junior Clemson was a total jerk, even if he was captain of the basketball team, and the sheriff's son *and* until today practically her best friend in the whole world ever since kindergarten.

And if this man made her cry she was never going to forgive him. *Never.*

"Suits you," the object of her fury muttered dryly under his breath. "Well then, Miss Sunshine—"

"Look, it's *Sunny,* all right? Sunny Severn."

"All right... Sunny." There was a pause. Sunny could feel those weird eyes looking at her. "You want to tell me now why you were running away?"

She shrugged and said with a bravado she didn't feel, "Who said I was running away?"

He made a sound that might have been a chuckle, if there had been any real amusement in it. "Right. You were going to visit your aunt in Los Angeles. Is that why you're so eager to see the sheriff? Perhaps we should ask—"

"All right, all right. *Geez,* I just wanted to get out of this stupid town, okay? I hate it here!"

"Why? It seems like a nice enough place. Do you think the grass will be greener somewhere else?"

Stubbornly keeping her head averted, Sunny muttered to her knotted hands, "I just don't belong here, okay?"

"And you think you belong in Los Angeles?"

"No! I don't know. So maybe I don't, so what?" Sunny paused, then added in a whisper, "I don't belong anywhere."

There was a long silence. When the man spoke again his voice sounded almost gentle. As if he sympathized. Sunny didn't dare look at his face to find out. "What about your family? Your mother and father? Don't you think they're probably worried about you?"

Sunny's body felt stiff. She jerked her head back to the window. "My father's dead."

"Your mother, then."

"My mother?" She laughed and brushed at her cheek with a quick, furtive movement, praying the man wouldn't notice. Sarge noticed, though, and nudged her hand with his nose in mute sympathy. "*She* doesn't care," Sunny muttered as she watched the first lights of Pinetree shimmer and dance beyond the car window. "She probably doesn't even know I'm gone."

Ann Severn deliberately turned her back on her reflection in the dark window and leaned, half-sitting, against the arm of the sofa. Her throat felt tight, and she rubbed it mechanically as she spoke into the telephone. "I don't know what to think, Bill. She's never been this late before."

The silence on the other end of the line was eloquent. She knew what the deputy sheriff was thinking, he'd told her often enough. You're too easy on that girl, Annie. She's had you jumping through hoops since she was twelve.

But all he said was, "You checked with all her friends?"

Friends? Sunny didn't have any friends that Ann knew of, not close ones, girlfriends she'd be likely to stay overnight with. Still, Ann had called everyone she could think of, just in case.

"No one's seen her," she said. "Not since school. She's been home, though." Her books were in a pile on the coffee table, where she'd dumped them out of her backpack. And she'd made herself a peanut butter sandwich and left the mess on the kitchen table. "Bill?" Ann took a deep breath. "She's taken all her money. She had maybe forty or fifty dollars in baby-sitting and birthday money, and it's gone. And she took Sarge."

Bill Clemson chuckled. "Well, shoot, then she couldn't have gone too far. She'd have to carry that poor old dog." Hearing Ann's silence, he stopped chuckling and sighed instead. "You want me to put something out on her? Annie, you know I can do that, but if I make it official it's going to go on her record. You sure you want that?" There was a thoughtful pause. "Now, if you ask me, it might not be a bad idea at that. Personally, I think what that kid needs is to get her butt—"

"Sunny is just going through a difficult stage," Ann said, closing her eyes and pressing her fingers hard against one tight temple. "Adolescence is hard enough on a child. She just needs patience and understanding—"

"Patience, hell! What that kid needs is some discipline. I may be way outa line here, but—"

"Someone's coming," Ann cut in, gripping the receiver so hard it hurt her hand as she watched the pattern of car lights and shrubbery shadows advance across the living room walls. "I think she's home. Thanks, Bill, I'm sorry I bothered you." She heard the sheriff swear as she placed the receiver on its cradle.

The headlights came slowly along the dark street. Ann watched them as if mesmerized, counting the heartbeats that thumped against her chest, pressing a hand over her mouth and hugging herself. A car, one she'd never seen before, eased to a stop at the front gate. The door on the passenger side opened, illuminating its occupants. Sunny, her only child, safe and sound.

In something like panic she thought, I don't know what to say to her! And then: My God, what's the matter with me? I think I'm afraid of my own child.

Three figures emerged from the car and came up the walk: Sunny first, head down, with Sarge shuffling gamely at her heels, and behind them a stranger, a big man whose face was hidden from her as he paused and leaned down to latch the gate behind them. His movements were graceful, his pace unhurried, a sharp contrast to Sunny's headlong march, which telegraphed her anger and resentment in every step.

Ann pushed away from the couch and moved to the door, her own steps jerky with relief. She took a deep breath and reached for the doorknob. "Sunny, where have you—"

But Sunny blew past her, bumping Ann's arm with her backpack as she went. A moment later her bedroom door slammed, rattling windows. Sarge sank with a groan into his favorite spot in the soft dirt beside the front steps, leaving Ann alone to face the stranger who had brought her daughter home.

My God, Rankin thought, is this the mother? She didn't look old enough to be *anybody's* mother—barely fifteen herself, standing in the open doorway in a blue bathrobe and bare feet, soft brown hair held back with some kind of band—or was it a ribbon? Everything about her seemed soft—soft brown eyes slightly tilted, a warm flush of distress on cheeks scrubbed clean as a child's, a generous mouth with a smile as transparent and winsome as a soap bubble, and as transient. He watched the smile evaporate and felt a sharp and unexpected sense of loss.

As he started up the steps he saw the first flicker of alarm in her eyes, and then the growing fear. The look wasn't new to him. A woman he'd once known had told him his own eyes could either charm or chill. What was it she'd said? You wear emotions like tinted glasses, *chérie*...without them your eyes are empty. That observation had never troubled him before, but for some reason it did now, and he took care to fill his eyes with his smile.

"Mrs. Severn?" He paused with one foot on the top step while he waited for her murmur of confirmation, and then decided to stay there so he wouldn't tower over her. He gestured in the direction of the recently slammed door. "And you are...Sunny's mother."

She nodded. "Yes. Thank you for bringing her home. I've been worried." And then, hugging her arms tightly across the front of her bathrobe, she straightened and almost seemed to grow taller. "Is she all right? What happened? She seems..."

Thoroughly dedicated now to erasing that look of fear in the woman's eyes, Rankin gave a wry, easy chuckle. "I'm afraid she's rather unhappy at the moment. She didn't care much for the choices I gave her."

"Choices?" She gave her head a confused shake, causing one thick wing of blunt-cut hair to slip forward over her shoulder.

Rankin found himself gazing at it as he explained, "I offered to bring her here, to you, or to the local police station."

"The *police*?" One hand clutched at the front of the blue robe. Rankin's eyes, drawn by that movement, caught the small convulsive ripple in her throat. "Why?" she asked in a voice flat with dread. "What did she do?"

"She was hitchhiking."

Sunny's mother whispered, "Oh, God," and turned and walked back into her living room, as if she'd forgotten that Rankin was there.

After a moment's hesitation he followed, taking the time to close the front door behind him. He wasn't sure why he did; he'd already accomplished what he'd intended, which was to return one smart-mouthed teenaged runaway to the bosom of her family—for the time being, at least. As unhappy as that girl obviously was, he had no doubt in his mind that she'd soon try it again. Which, he reminded himself, was none of his concern. He needed to be on his way; if he pushed it he could still make it to Joseph Varga's tonight, though not, perhaps, at what would be considered a polite hour. So he was somewhat surprised to hear himself address the woman's back in conversational tones.

"You don't happen to have a sister living in Los Angeles, do you?"

She turned, rubbing distractedly at her temple. "No, no one. Why?"

"I just wondered. That's where your daughter said she wanted to go."

The woman digested that in absolute silence, staring at him, chin high, her back held very straight. Even so, Rankin thought, the top of her head probably wouldn't reach his— The idea startled him, so he shut it off. It was a comparison that he knew wouldn't ordinarily occur to him, one that he found troubling in indefinable ways.

The tiny muscles around her eyes flinched slightly, as if she'd felt a spasm of pain. "She was...running away?"

Rankin nodded. "Apparently." And then, to break a long and anguished silence he said gently, "Do you have any idea why she would want to?"

She shook her head and quickly turned her back to him, lifting her hand to her face in a way that would have seemed casual to most observers. But as an observer there was nothing casual about Rankin, and he recognized the gesture for what it was; he'd seen the daughter make one just like it a little earlier, in the car.

"No," she said in a flat, careful voice, "Sunny doesn't confide in me...." She frowned at him over her shoulder. "I'm sorry, I don't know your name."

"Oh— I'm sorry. It's Rankin." He held out his hand. And when he felt her small hand take his in a warm, surprisingly firm grasp, he heard himself giving her something he seldom gave to anyone, and never, ever to strangers: "*Niall* Rankin."

Two

———

His hand was big and warm, and his eyes, which a moment ago had seemed so cold, now were reassuring. Ann felt the icy knot in her stomach begin to melt and loosen. Vivid memories of another night, another unfamiliar car, another knock on her door slowly faded. It wasn't the same, she told herself. Sunny was right here, in the next room, angry but safe and sound. It was going to be all right. She could handle this. After Mark she could handle anything.

Shaking off her fear along with the dead, dry remnants of the past, she smiled up at the man who'd brought her daughter back to her. "Mine's Ann," she said. "I haven't seen you around. You must be new."

And yet she found herself searching his face, looking for some familiar point of reference that might explain the sudden feeling that she *knew* him. Odd, when everything about him was foreign to her, from the casual elegance of the clothes he wore to the softly sibilant cadence of his accent.

"New?" He'd been staring at her, too, she realized, with a curious intensity that made her wonder if she had a smudge of something on her nose. He frowned and shook his head, sounding puzzled and slightly distracted. "No, I'm afraid I'm not from anywhere around here."

His voice seemed to come from a great distance. As if, she thought, there was a kind of curtain around her mind, shutting her inside herself with her own private impressions. A blizzard of impressions that confused her senses and clouded her judgment. It was a moment before his words penetrated that curtain, but when they did, their meaning was enough to dissipate it completely. She pulled her hand from his and stepped back, all at once alert to the fact that there was a large, strange man in her house.

"You're not one of Bill's deputies," she said, trying not to let him see her unease. "What are you, then—some kind of juvenile officer?"

At that the man smiled, making his eyes crease at the corners and giving his harsh features an oddly poignant charm. "No, no—nothing like that. I was on my way to Los Angeles when I saw your daughter trying to hitch a ride. That struck me as dangerous, if not outright insane, so I stopped, picked her up and brought her home. That's all. I'm not a policeman." The thought seemed to amuse him.

Ann felt herself relaxing again, though why that should be so she couldn't imagine, because if he wasn't a cop, then she really did have a man in her house she didn't know from Adam. It was that smile of his, she thought. It was as contagious as a winter cold. "Well, I should have known that," she said, succumbing to it and giving him back one of her own. "I went to school with pretty near all the peace officers in this town."

"You've lived here all your life, then?" It was a casual question, a polite question, the kind strangers ask each other, but he asked it as if he really wanted the answer, as if it were important for him to know.

"Yeah," Ann said, with a slightly apologetic shrug. "I was born here. What about you? Where...um—" She paused, natural curiosity battling good manners. "I was wondering about...you know, your accent."

"I was born in Germany."

"Ah," Ann said, nodding. "Germany." It was a conversational dead end. She waited, but he didn't offer anything more, and of course she couldn't ask. She'd sensed a change in him at her question, the slightest hint of withdrawal, and growing up in a place where everyone knew everyone else and neighbors were apt to be neighbors for a lifetime, her respect for privacy was ingrained.

So, after a moment of awkward silence, she cleared her throat and said, "Well—" just as her unexpected guest looked at his watch and said, "I guess I'd better be on my way."

Something inside her gave an involuntary leap of protest. "Oh—" she said, and then stopped. He waited, one eyebrow lifted, for her to continue. She felt her cheeks grow warm as she heard herself saying things she couldn't account for, things she'd never imagined she would ever say to a stranger.

"Listen, can I get you a cup of coffee or something before you go? It's the least I can do, after you went so far out of your way to bring Sunny home, and now it's so late, and it's a long way to L.A., and there's probably nothing open in town, except maybe the bar at the Buckhorn, and that's apt to be pretty rowdy this time of night. It'd only take a minute, if you don't mind instant—"

"Thank you." The man's ice-blue gaze had been roaming the living room, examining its modest furnishings with the mild curiosity of a tourist in a museum. When he brought it back to Ann she felt it like a physical touch, cutting off her babbling in mid-sentence. "That would be nice," he said quietly. "Instant is fine. Black, please, with sugar."

"Sugar," Ann repeated, suddenly at a loss, and as breathless as if she'd run a race.

She managed to pull herself together enough to offer to take his coat and to tell him to make himself comfortable on the couch, but she didn't invite him into her kitchen. She told herself it was because it was so small, that he would feel cramped and umcomfortable there. She left the door open, though, and while she was running water into the teakettle, setting it on the stove, turning the gas on under it and assembling things on a small tray, she kept stealing glances through it at the man who said his name was—what was it? Oh, yes. *Neal.* Neal Rankin.

He hadn't taken the seat on the couch she'd suggested, but instead was wandering the room, pausing to pick up a knickknack and put it down again, leaning over to examine the pictures on the walls. The one of Ann, taken the day she graduated from high school, standing in front of the red rose bush in the yard; Grandma and Grandpa's wedding picture; the collage of snapshots of Sunny as a baby, a toddler, a smiling little girl; the one of Daddy in his rodeo days, sitting on his favorite roping horse, the buckskin named Yeller.

It gave her a strange feeling, having him prowl through her life and memories like that. There was a tightness in her stomach she didn't want to admit was excitement...or even fear.

He moves so easily, she thought, so gracefully for such a big man. But with a certain wariness, too, that reminded her of something she couldn't quite recall. It nagged at the edges of her memory while she studied him, looking for something in the angle of his head, the set of his shoulders, a mannerism or a gesture that would nudge the picture into focus. But it wasn't until she was climbing up onto the counter to get a cup from the top shelf where she kept Grandma's good china—checking first to make sure her guest wasn't going to catch her doing it—that it finally came to her.

It had been when she was very small, when her mother was alive and they were still spending Christmases with Grandma and Grandpa, before Grandpa sold the ranch and moved south to Phoenix for the sake of Grandma's health. On that unforgettable Christmas Eve, Grandpa had gotten her out of her warm bed, motioning her to silence with a finger to his lips, and carried her through the cold, dark house to the front window. It had snowed the day before, and with the moon high in the sky it had seemed almost as bright as day, but a day without colors, only black and white.

And gray. One silvery-gray moving shadow.

Cozy in a warm quilt, with Grandpa's arms around her, Ann had watched the mountain lion prowl through the yard, circling the barn and the empty corrals, pausing to sniff around the chicken house, now locked up tight, its occupants sleeping, oblivious to the presence of the predator. The cougar had seemed like a ghost to her, silent as smoke, scary and beautiful at the same time, moving so gracefully and yet so cautiously through a world that wasn't his.

Yes, and she'd felt the same thing then, the same shivery tightness inside her that was part excitement, part awe, part fear.

In the morning, Grandpa and Daddy and the hired man had taken guns and followed the tracks in the snow, around the barnyard and across the meadow and into the timber beyond. But the lion was gone, and they never saw him again....

"Is that *tea*, by any chance?" He had come, silent as a cat, to fill the doorway.

Startled, nerves jumping, Ann followed his gaze to the open cupboard, and the brightly colored box on the lowest shelf. She nodded, clutching Grandma's china cup to her chest and trying to act as if it was perfectly normal for her to be standing on the kitchen counter. "It's lemon spice herbal, no caffeine. But I probably have some regular tea bags somewhere, if you'd rather—"

"I don't suppose you'd have any Darjeeling around, would you?" There was a wistful note in his voice.

"No...sorry," Ann said with a shrug of apology. She'd never even *heard* of it.

"Ah well..." His smile was wry. "Never mind. Coffee's fine." He folded his arms on his broad chest and leaned against the doorframe.

Ann waited for him to go back to the living room, but he seemed content to stay where he was, watching her with great interest, and what she was certain was great amusement. She was suddenly too aware of her bathrobe and the nightgown under it, and the fact that she wasn't wearing underwear, too aware of the cold counter tile under her bare feet.

She cleared her throat nervously. He straightened at once, looking solicitous, and said, "Do you need help?"

Before she could reply she felt his hands on her waist and found herself looking straight down into a pair of glittering blue eyes. It was a strange perspective for someone who was barely five feet tall. It made her head swim. She gasped and clutched Grandma's china and his broad shoulders as she was lifted from the counter and set with mortifying ease upon the floor.

"Thank you," she said primly, as soon as her equilibrium had returned.

"Don't mention it," he murmured, taking his hands from her waist.

For an instant she wished them back on her again as she discovered that her legs had inexplicably become unreliable. "It will...um... It'll be just a minute," she said, unobtrusively putting a hand on the countertop to steady herself. "If you'd like to just make yourself comfortable..."

He made *her* uncomfortable. He gave her claustrophobia, which was silly, because she knew his attention wasn't even focused on her any longer. His gaze was roaming the kitchen with that same casual curiosity with which he'd examined the living room, touching on the white-ruffled curtains, the African violet on the windowsill, the refrigerator magnets made from Sunny's soccer photos, and the plaster cast of Sunny's handprint from kindergarten that hung on the wall beside the back door. As if, Ann thought, he'd never seen anything like them before.

The teakettle's shriek was a relief. Her guest straightened and said, "Ah." Ann turned off the gas and poured water over the mound of brown crystals in the bottom of the cup, stirred, and then picked up the tray. She meant to carry it into the living room, but he took it from her and placed it on the table instead. She hesitated, then turned back to the counter and mixed water and coffee in her favorite mug, the one Sunny had given her for Mother's Day several years ago, that said "World's Greatest Mom" on it in about twenty different languages. As she carried it to the tiny table beside the window she noticed that her guest was stroking a leaf of the African violet with a forefinger. He smiled and looked up at her as she sat down.

"The caffeine won't bother you?" he asked. "Keep you awake? You don't have to drive to Los Angeles tonight."

Ann murmured absently, "No, not really." She had barely heard him, because she was suddenly mesmerized by his hands.

She hadn't noticed them before; even shaking hands with him she'd been aware only of their warmth, of their size and strength. And when he'd placed them on her waist, she'd thought of nothing at all. Now, as she watched them spoon sugar, stir coffee and cradle her grandmother's delicate china, it struck her that they were completely at odds with the rest of him.

He seemed all elegance, from his dark, finely molded head with the wings of silver at the temples to the toes of his soft leather shoes. She'd had him pegged as rich, probably born to it, and a sophisticated city man through and through. But somewhere along the line those hands of his had taken a beating. They were weathered and gnarled, and several of the fingers looked as if they'd been broken and badly set. Her grandfather had had hands like that, and so had her father, but she'd never seen scars quite like these, up high, just below the wrists....

She wanted to know about those scars. She wanted to know about this man called Neal Rankin, and how he'd come to have hands like an old cowhand. She was trying to overcome her ingrained reluctance to pry when she suddenly realized that he'd asked *her* a question, and was waiting politely for an answer.

"I'm sorry," she said, covering her embarrassment with a sip of coffee. "What did you say?"

His smile was wry, as if he knew exactly what she'd been thinking about. "I asked if you have to get up early in the morning." He gestured with his head, indicating the way she was dressed. "You were obviously ready to go to bed."

"Oh...well." Ann had a sudden and vivid reprise of the feel of his hands on her waist. She looked down at herself and plucked self-consciously at the sleeve of her robe. I look like a frump, she thought, much too aware of his eyes on her, wondering why she cared when in a few minutes, no more, he was going to get in his car and drive away. Forever.

She placed her coffee mug firmly on the tablecloth in front of her and kept her eyes on it while she answered. "I do get up early, but more for Sunny than for me. She has to be in school by eight, and sometimes it's a little hard for her to get going in the morning. I don't have to be at work until nine. I work in a bank, Sierra National, down on Main Street." His eyes were still on her—she could feel them. "It's...just kitty-corner from the Buckhorn." She drank coffee to stop herself from talking.

There was a long pause. "Sunny told me her father is dead."

"Yes."

"I'm sorry."

Ann got up and carried her cup to the sink, turning her back on those all-seeing eyes. "It was twelve years ago," she said with a dismissive shrug, hoping to close the subject.

But he wouldn't let it go. "It's difficult raising a child alone," he said softly in a voice that spoke of first-hand knowledge. Ann's throat tightened.

She took a deep breath and lifted her head, but couldn't trust herself to turn around. "It hasn't always been," she said lightly. "Sunny is just having...a difficult adolescence. You know how it is."

"No, I can't say that I do." His voice was flat now; she must have imagined that moment of sympathy. Nerves shivered down her back as she heard the clink of china and felt him come up behind her, reach past her to place his coffee cup beside hers in the sink. And then...the lightest of touches on her elbow. "You've been very kind," he said formally, "but it's time I let you go to bed. Thank you for the coffee."

"You're welcome," Ann murmured automatically. When he'd moved as far as the kitchen doorway and she could breathe again, she gulped in air and followed him, babbling earnestly. "Listen—thank you. Thank you again—for picking Sunny up and bringing her home. I don't know what would have happened if—"

He held up his hand as if to shut off the flow of words. "Don't mention it." His smile seemed slightly off-center. "Good night." A moment later he was gone.

In her room, in the dark, midnight stillness, Sunny heard the front door close. Every nerve in her body tensed, listening.

He's gone, she thought. *Now* she'll come.

Even under the piled-up blankets she was shivering, a small, cold knot of misery. She'd cried a little, earlier, but had stopped when she'd realized there was no one to hear her, no one to care. *Nobody* cares, she told herself; that was the sad but unavoidable truth. Her mother wasn't even angry with her, which didn't really surprise her. Her mother never got mad about anything, not even the D Sunny was getting in math. Sunny hadn't told her yet about the failing grade in P.E., just because of that stupid shirt which wasn't even her fault but nobody cared about that either.

And then there was the other thing, the reason she just couldn't go back to school tomorrow, or ever, ever again. She'd die if she had to face those...jerks again—really *die*. If only, she thought, there was someone she could talk to. But there was no one she could tell about this—least of all her mother.

She lay still, not even breathing, listening to her heart beat, listening to the quiet sounds her mother made, locking the front door, turning off the lights.

Now, she thought. Maybe *now* she'll come.

She lay rigid, listening so hard her head hurt, listening to her mother's footsteps in the hallway, the sigh of the turning doorknob, the faintest squeak of hinges. Light from the hall threw a narrow rectangle across her bedroom floor.

"Sunny," her mother called softly, "are you awake?"

Sunny closed her eyes and held her breath, waiting... waiting. After a few moments she heard the gentle click of the closing door, and the sound her mother's bare feet made on the hardwood floor of the hallway.

Warm tears oozed out from under her eyelashes and ran down into her hair.

Rankin stood on Ann Severn's front doorstep and wished with all his heart and soul for a cigarette. After the warmth of the house the night air felt cold to him and smelled sweet, like some kind of flower. He inhaled deeply as he shrugged into his jacket, and decided that it must be lilacs.

Behind him the light in the living room window winked out, leaving him with a sky full of stars, a pale strip of pathway leading to a gate in a picket fence and beyond that an unlighted street leading to a long lonely stretch of desert highway. And beyond that, of course, was Los Angeles, which was a different kind of lonely.

As Rankin went down the steps the old dog stirred and thumped the ground with his stub of a tail. "Well, trouper, how are you?" Rankin murmured, pausing to rub the shaggy black head. "Tired?" The dog gave a great sigh and laid his muzzle back down on his paws. Rankin chuckled. "Yeah...I know how you feel."

He gave the dog a farewell pat, got his hand licked in return, then straightened and strode with purpose down the walk and through the gate in the picket fence. He got into his rental car and drove down the dark street to the highway, where he turned left at the caution light, then left again into the driveway of a motel called the Whispering Pines Lodge.

He told himself that he was tired, and that Los Angeles would still be there in the morning. Tomorrow he would get up early, consume yet another greasy fried-egg breakfast and battery acid coffee and be on his way. The episode of the widow Severn and her wayward daughter Sunny was just another small glitch in an otherwise monotonous, and apparently pointless, journey. It would soon be forgotten. These people were none of his concern, and he would put them both immediately and forever out of his mind....

But even before he'd opened his eyes the next morning he knew that his last conscious thought had been of Ann. It was her face he'd seen, projected on the backs of his eyelids, as he'd drifted at last into sleep—her sweet-scrubbed skin, the small cluster of freckles on her narrow-bridged nose, the hint of a dimple when she smiled, gentle brown eyes and soft brown hair. The feel of her body between his hands, the intriguing play of thick fabric over something clinging and slippery...was like a stain he couldn't wash off.

Ann... Everything about her was soft—soft to the ears, the touch, the mind. Even in his hard slab of a motel room bed he'd felt her softness, and it had warmed and soothed him, like a roaring fire and a glass of brandy on a cold night.

It was that warmth that had drawn him, he decided, which was entirely understandable, given his frame of mind at the time. It had been a long time since he'd held a woman in his arms, and even longer since he'd been intrigued by one. He'd been tired, fed up with traveling, and she and her cozy little small-town nest had seemed like an oasis to him. A temporary refuge, nothing more. Ann Severn and her life-style were as alien to him as he and his undoubtedly were to her.

He couldn't account as easily for the sense of recognition that had come over him there in her kitchen, later, in that instant before she'd turned her back to him, shielding her eyes from him. And he couldn't account at all for the sense of banishment he'd felt when he left her. Always a wanderer, he thought, giving in to a momentary twinge of self-pity. Always beyond the pale.

He was still thinking about it when he walked into the Buckhorn Café. And frowning, which was probably why the waitress going by with a coffeepot in one hand and a plate of ham and eggs in the other gave him a quick glance, and then a longer look accompanied by a somewhat nervous smile. In spite of it, she sang out a friendly, "Hi there. Have a seat, and I'll be with you in just a minute."

Rankin took a small table in the back of the room as was his habit, so that he could have a clear view of the room and whoever came and went in it. It had been a while since such precautions had been vital to his health and longevity, but old habits die hard.

The waitress arrived with the coffeepot in her hand and purpose in her eye. "You look like a man who could use a good cuppa coffee," she proclaimed as she turned the heavy ceramic mug in front of Rankin right-side up.

"Actually," Rankin said hurriedly, repressing a shudder as he eyed the oily black liquid that was quivering on the lip of the pot, "what I could really use is a good cup of tea. Or even a bad one, for that matter. You wouldn't, by any chance, have a tea bag around?"

"Boy, I'm battin' zero this mornin'," the waitress said cheerfully. "Tea it is. And what else can I get for you, sir?"

"Perhaps a menu," Rankin suggested, without sarcasm. He'd already observed that most of the Buckhorn's clientele appeared to be regulars, who ordered by muttering, "Gimme the usual," as they groped for their first cup of coffee.

The waitress snatched a well-thumbed menu from a pocket at the end of the counter and presented it to him with a brisk, "There you go, sir, and I'll be right back with your tea."

Rankin watched her work her way through the tables, refilling coffee cups, chatting with customers in her loud, breezy voice about the weather, or business, or the basketball game that had been played in the local high school gymnasium the previous Friday, and which the home team had evidently won. He decided he liked her. She had probably been very pretty once, and was still handsome, although in a few more years the smoker's lines around her eyes and mouth would make her old before her time. But she had a spontaneous smile and friendly eyes, and probably not a mean or devious bone in her body. He wondered what the letters "B.J." monogrammed on the pocket of her uniform stood for. When she brought him his pitcher of hot water and tea bag he thought about asking her, and it surprised him to realize that he really wanted to know.

He ordered his usual ham and eggs straight up and sourdough toast and left the question unasked, knowing it would tease his imagination for a little while. Betty Jo? Bobby Jean? But it really didn't matter, after all. After today he'd never see the waitress—or any of these people—again.

The front door of the Buckhorn whisked opened and then shut. The creak of leather and clank of hardware identified the newcomer for Rankin even before he'd glanced up from the tea bag he was dipping methodically up and down in a little ceramic pitcher of hot water. He'd never met a uniformed law officer yet who could move quietly.

The waitress sang out, "Mornin', Bill. Be with you in a sec."

There was a chorus of greetings and good-natured ribbing from the other diners.

"Well, would you look what the coyotes dragged in!"

"Uh-oh, hide the cards, Ed."

"Geez, if it ain't the proud papa hisself."

"Yeah, say, that was one helluva game, wasn't it? What was it your boy Will had? Thirty-two points?"

"Thirty-two, hell, that was just the first half!"

"Nah, it was thirty-seven."

"Come on, thirty-seven? That's gotta be pretty close to Mark Severn's record, ain't it?"

"What about it, Bill? That boy of yours decided where he's gonna play ball next year?"

The sheriff fielded all the comments with a grin and a wave, and muttered, "B.J., give me a cup of that coffee, will you?" as he straddled a stool at the counter. His manner was relaxed and casual, but all Rankin's instincts were humming at high volume. He'd bet his life the lawman was there for a purpose, and it wasn't the coffee.

Rankin sat with the menu in front of him and studied the sheriff out of the corner of his eye. Tall...lanky... easygoing, with thinning blond hair and the kind of skin that burned in the sun. And from the looks of things, it had been getting more sun exposure than was good for it recently; either that, or the sheriff had a tendency to blush. Deceptive, Rankin decided. That boyish look and lazy manner might cause some people to underestimate him, to their ultimate sorrow. Rankin wouldn't make that mistake. He'd learned long ago never to judge a man by his appearance.

"Got any of that apple pie this morning?" the sheriff inquired as he watched the waitress pour his coffee.

"Sure do, hon," B.J. chirped with an engaging little wiggle. "You know I'd save you a piece."

"Warm it up for me, will you?"

"Will do."

The sheriff swiveled his stool around and stood up, carrying his coffee mug with him. A moment later the chair across from Rankin scraped back and a quiet voice said, "Mind if I join you?"

Rankin looked up, feigning surprise. "Not at all." He made a show of rearranging his teapot to make room. "Something I can do for you, Sheriff?"

The sheriff settled himself, took a sip of coffee and made a face that seemed to indicate he was in extreme pain. "Ah, boy, that coffee sure hits the spot, doesn't it?" He stuck out his hand. "Bill Clemson."

Rankin shook hands and murmured, "Rankin."

The sheriff nodded, took a piece of paper out of his shirt pocket, glanced at it and poked it back in its place. "You're a long way from home, Mr. Rankin." He drank coffee, grimaced and shook his head. "We don't get too many rental cars with Virginia plates through here."

Rankin knew better than to ask. He let the seconds tick by while he poured himself a cup of tea, lifted it, blew on it and drank. He set the cup carefully back in its saucer and said mildly, "Tell me, do you run a check on every traveler that passes through your town, Sheriff?"

Before he could answer, B.J. arrived with both their orders. When she had gone away again, Bill Clemson frowned at his, then said to Rankin, "You wanna hand me that pitcher of half-n-half, there?" Rankin obliged. The sheriff poured half its contents over the steaming pie, explaining as he did so, "Can't take those yellow eyes staring up at me in the morning, know what I mean? And I figure this beats the hell out of oatmeal." He forked a generous bite into his mouth, chewed and shook his head. "Ah, man, that's good. Now—what was it you were asking?" He poked his fork in Rankin's direction. "Oh, yeah. Do I check out every stranger that comes to town." He chuckled and dug into his pie. "Now, that'd be pretty impractical. No...no, I pretty much just concentrate on the ones that interest me."

"I see," Rankin said, lifting one eyebrow to express amusement and mild surprise. "I can't imagine what there is about me that would interest you. I'm simply...passing through."

The sheriff grinned, all shiny teeth and hard eyes "You've just got that kind of face, I guess. Sort of makes a lawman nervous, know what I mean?'' The smile disappeared along with the last forkful of pie. Bill Clemson pushed the empty plate aside. ''Plus,'' he said softly, ''Ann Severn happens to be a good friend of mine.''

''Ah,'' Rankin said, and was aware of a faint twinge of disappointment. A jealous boyfriend—he should have guessed. ''Well, as I said, I'm just passing through, so you don't have anything to worry about.''

The sheriff picked up his magically refilled coffee mug and sat back in his chair with a sigh. ''Mr. Rankin, I assure you I've got plenty of things to worry about—'' he drank, grimaced, and gestured with the mug ''—but I don't think you're going to be one of 'em. I'll know for sure when I get the full word from Virginia. Shouldn't be long now, but I'm not too concerned. Hell, I've got to worry about budget cuts in my department, a face-off between some animal lovers and the Bureau of Land Management over the tule elk, and one of my dispatchers is down with the flu. On top of that, I've got a bunch of religious crazies sitting up in the mountains in bunkers waiting for Judgment Day.'' He swore under his breath. The look he leveled at Rankin was cool, intelligent, frankly appraising . . . and something else. It was obvious the sheriff hadn't been lying when he'd said he was worried.

''You brought Sunny home last night,'' he said. It wasn't a question.

Rankin nodded. ''That's right.''

''Mind telling me how you happened to do that, seeing as how you were 'just passing through'?''

''Not at all,'' Rankin said easily. ''I found her hitchhiking and picked her up. And then I gave her a choice between her place or yours.''

''Hitchhiking.'' The sheriff swore again, aloud this time, and ran a hand over what was left of his hair. ''Where was she?''

''On the highway,'' Rankin said. ''About ten miles south of here.''

"South." Bill Clemson let out his breath in what sounded to Rankin like a sigh of relief. "How was she? Did she say where she was going, or why? Did she seem . . . you know, upset?"

"Upset?" Rankin lifted an eyebrow. "She was hitch-hiking on a dark desert highway in the middle of the night." He poured his tea, taking his time about it, and when he had it to his liking glanced up at the sheriff and said bluntly, "Look, I'm a stranger here. If you're concerned about Sunny, why don't you talk to someone who knows her a little bit better? Her mother, for instance."

"Ann? Naw, she won't tell me anything." The sheriff gave a short, unhappy laugh. "She already thinks I'm being an overprotective big brother."

"Brother," said Rankin thoughtfully.

"Yeah, Annie and I go back a long way." Apparently reassured by Rankin's relaxed attitude and the information he'd offered, Clemson was shedding the constraints of his profession almost visibly. "Grew up together. Annie's husband Mark was my best friend. We used to double date a lot, Mark and Ann, Patty—that's my wife—and I. I was best man at their wedding. He would have been at mine, but he was already in Nam, and we . . . well we couldn't afford to wait until he got back, if you know what I mean." He coughed, and his sunburn intensified slightly.

Rankin said, "Is that how he died, then? In Vietnam?"

"Mark? Nah, not him—he always did have a charmed life. Came back without a scratch, at least that's what we thought at the time. He and Ann got married right after he got back, and Sunny came along about a year later. They sure seemed happy. . . ." He paused, staring down into his coffee mug as he swirled its contents around and around.

"What happened?" asked Rankin softly.

Bill Clemson cleared his throat and shifted restlessly in his chair. "Ah, hell, I don't know. Mark just never was quite the same after he came back from Nam. I don't know what happened to him over there—after some of these movies I've seen, God only knows. But after he came home, he'd get moody sometimes, and when he did, you didn't want to be around him. Oh, I don't mean he'd get violent, or anything like that—he never laid a hand on Ann or Sunny—if he had I'd have laid him out myself, and he knew it. No, he'd just get in these black depressions, and he'd drink a lot. Sometimes he'd disappear for a few days, and Annie, she'd be out of her mind worrying about him.'' He paused again, and this time Rankin didn't prompt him.

He wasn't sure why the sheriff was telling him, a stranger, all this, but there were two things he'd learned in his lifetime that made him listen without questioning: one was that if you waited long enough, the answers usually came; the other was that sometimes the answers weren't what you expected.

The sheriff leaned forward, both arms resting on the tabletop, hands encircling the coffee mug as if drawing a measure of comfort from its warmth. His eyes looked beyond Rankin, into the past. ''It was twelve years ago—Sunny was just three. Mark went off on one of his toots, and the rumor around town was that he'd shacked up with a waitress that worked at the truck stop just north of town.'' He shook his head, looked down, then away, fidgeting in the way that strong men do when they are battling strong emotions. ''Then, about a week later, a couple of high school kids looking for a place to make out found their bodies up at the old rock quarry. He'd shot her first, then turned the gun on himself.''

''Casualties of war,'' murmured Rankin.

Three

"I'll never forget that night." Bill put one hand over his eyes and rubbed as if they hurt him. "I was green as grass, hadn't been with the department six months. I took the call." He gave a short, hollow laugh. "Ah...hell. You know what I was thinking about? He did it with an old thirty-eight. I don't know how many times we'd been up at that same quarry, the two of us, with the same damn gun, shooting at beer bottles, and me always kidding him about what a lousy shot he was.... Let me tell you, it took me— took all of us, the whole town—a long time to get over that. Mark was a hero around here, basketball star in high school, then the only local boy to go to Vietnam. People still talk about it."

"Must be hard on his widow," Rankin commented. "Living with the constant reminders."

"Annie's tougher than she looks. I think she probably handled it better than some of us did. Somehow or other, she picked up the pieces, put it all behind her and got on with her life. Of course, she had that little girl to raise...."

Bill picked up his check, took a pen out of his shirt pocket and scrawled a signature across it.

Rankin turned his check over and glanced at it. "I can't help but wonder," he said casually as he reached for his wallet, "how it's been for 'that little girl,' growing up with something like that hanging over her."

"The sins of the fathers, you mean?"

Rankin shrugged. "Seems to me it would have been better for her to move away from where it all happened, where it's common knowledge and the subject of everyone's conversation, and start over someplace else with a clean slate." He looked up from the bills he was counting out and added pointedly, "If she had, maybe that little girl wouldn't be trying to hitch a ride out of town with the first stranger that happens along."

There was a moment of tense silence, and then Bill said, "I've thought about that. I imagine Annie has, too." He pushed back his chair and stood up. Rankin did the same, and followed the sheriff through the maze of oilcloth-covered tables to the cash register. He paid his check while Bill bantered and flirted with B.J., and they left the Buckhorn Café together.

"Before you judge Ann for sticking around here," Bill said when they were standing on the sidewalk, squinting into the morning brilliance while he groped for his sunglasses, "let me tell you a little something about small towns. You ever live in a small town?" He glanced at Rankin and went on without waiting for his answer. "A small town, especially when you're born there, grow up there, isn't just a place to live. It's more like a home . . . a family. Now, if you've got family you're close to, when trouble comes you don't up and leave, you move in closer, know what I mean? You take your strength and comfort from the people that love you. That's something maybe people have gotten away from, the way the world is now. But this . . ." He drew in a breath and looked around him, surveying the wide street lined with neon motel signs and the snow-capped peaks of the Sierra Nevadas beyond. "This is Annie's home. She was born here. She belongs here, you understand?''

Rankin nodded, but he was hearing a voice full of adolescent hurt and confusion, a voice that had mirrored so clearly the feelings locked deep in his own heart that it scared him.

I just don't belong here. I don't belong anywhere.

"Tell me something," he said abruptly, watching a group of young people passing by on the other side of the street, dressed in the nondescript, vaguely disreputable manner of teenagers everywhere, laughing and talking, obviously on their way to school. "When I told you I'd picked Sunny up south of here, you seemed almost relieved. It seemed to me you expected her to be somewhere else, someplace you weren't happy about. Is that right?"

Bill snorted and shook his head. "Ah hell, I didn't want to worry Ann, but when she told me Sunny was missing, the first thing I thought of was that she'd gone up the mountain with those crazies."

Rankin frowned. "Any special reason why you think she'd do that?"

"Shoot, those people have been proselytizing all over town, handing out leaflets to our kids outside the high school—even catch 'em coming out of church. You take a kid with troubles, like Sunny, and somebody comes along claiming to have all the answers, it can sound pretty attractive."

"True," Rankin murmured. "Who are they, these people? What are they preaching that worries you so much?"

"Besides the imminent end of the world, you mean?" The sheriff made a frustrated sound. "I don't know, and that's what worries me. I got nothing against any religion, I swear to God, but any time three or four hundred strangers move into my jurisdiction, that interests me. And I ask you this, if they've got nothing to hide, what do they need a ten-foot high chain-link fence topped with barbed wire for, huh? I'm telling you, it looks like a damn concentration camp up there. Hell, if they want to sit and wait for Armageddon, that's fine with me, but if they have any ideas about helping it along, like those people in South America—you know, the ones that committed mass suicide?—they aren't going to do it in my territory. And they aren't going to take any of our young people along with 'em, not if I have anything to say about it. The trouble is, I can't get into that blasted compound of theirs. I haven't got cause—'' He broke off, swearing. ''Ah, geez, there's a couple of their people now, see that? With more of those damn leaflets.''

On the other side of the street, the group of teenagers was approaching the corner where the light now blinked red, forcing the highway traffic to let them cross. Several of the group were lagging behind, having been waylaid by two newcomers dressed in dark slacks and shirts so white they reflected the morning sun. Their hair, Rankin observed, was neatly trimmed. And they were wearing neckties.

''Those are your crazies?'' he said, lifting an eyebrow as the sheriff's sunburn deepened to a frustrated crimson. ''I was expecting sackcloth robes and shaved heads. They seem quite clean-cut to me.''

''Too clean-cut,'' Bill muttered. ''Call it instinct, call it whatever you like, but there's just something about those kids that isn't *right*. Now, you take a normal kid—take my boy, Will, for instance. He's a good kid, the best—works hard, gets good grades, has a real chance at a basketball scholarship to a top-notch school. Patty and I are real proud of him. But sometimes you'd like to wring his neck, you know what I mean? The kid can't walk through the house without leaving a trail of litter behind him. He'd rather wear pants with holes in 'em than anything else, and getting him to cut his hair is like pulling teeth. What I'm sayin' is, he's normal. *Those* kids, now, they're like a bunch of robots. Give me the creeps.''

Rankin watched the young people across the street with narrowed, thoughtful eyes. He made no comment.

The sheriff's beeper went off and he silenced it with a muttered oath, then grinned at Rankin. ''Well, that's the report I've been waiting for, what'll you bet? When did you say you were planning on leaving town?''

Rankin grinned back. "Soon, I guess, unless there's something in that report I don't know about.''

"Well, it's been nice talkin' to you," Bill said, transferring his keys to his left hand and holding out his right. Rankin took it, and felt keen-eyed appraisal, even from behind the dark aviator glasses. "Listen, I want to thank you for bringing Sunny home. You come back sometime when you feel like stayin' awhile, and I'll promise you the best trout fishing this side of the Rockies."

"You've got a deal," Rankin said, and was surprised by the ring of sincerity in his own voice. What was it about this town, these people, he wondered, that made him feel as if he'd known them for years? He had good instincts about people and generally formed conclusions about them pretty quickly. He'd pegged Bill Clemson as one of the good guys right from the first, and he knew that if he were ever in a tight spot, he'd be glad to have the sheriff on his side. But he'd formed very few friendships in his lifetime, and the ones he did have—Joseph Varga's included—had developed over long periods of time. He couldn't account for the sudden idea that standing in a wilderness stream up to his waders in icy cold snowmelt with a local law officer might be something he'd very much enjoy doing.

After the cream-colored sedan with the sheriff's insignia on the door had disappeared around the corner beyond the Buckhorn, Rankin shook off a vague sense of regret and then, instead of heading back to the Whispering Pines lodge, waited for a break in traffic and jogged across the highway. The high school kids were long gone on their way to school and the two young delegates from the religious colony had disappeared, but several of their leaflets lay where they'd been discarded, one in the gutter, one flapping against a fence, another scooting slowly along the sidewalk at the whim of a breeze. Rankin picked one up, skimmed through it, and frowned. He read it again, more slowly, and thought of Bill Clemson's words.

Gives me the creeps.

He knew a lot about propaganda and mind control and brain washing. Too much. He thought about what Bill had said about the young people from the religious colony being like robots, and in spite of the warm spring sunshine, he felt a chill.

But it was Bill Clemson's problem, not his, Rankin reminded himself even as he was carefully folding the leaflet and putting it in his jacket pocket. These people, Bill, Ann, Sunny, their past tragedies and present troubles, were none of his concern. He had places to go, people to see... decisions to make. The past wasn't important; he'd come to terms with his and put it behind him long ago. What mattered was the present—and the future. And there was a good chance his own future was waiting for him right now, in L.A.

As he was walking back to the Whispering Pines Motel, Rankin noticed the bank where Ann worked, "catty-corner across from the Buckhorn." He glanced at his watch, thinking that it was too early for her to be there yet, trying to imagine Ann Severn sitting behind a desk, dressed in a neat dark suit, with her hair pulled back in a bun. The thought made him smile. No way. He was always going to remember her in a blue robe and bare feet, with a ribbon in her hair. And he *would* remember her, and Sunny, too. There was no doubt of that in his mind at all.

He stopped in the motel office and paid his bill, then went to his room to collect his things. It didn't take long—he'd only carried in the small overnighter with his shaving things and a change of underwear—and by this time he had the checking-out process down to a science.

The morning sun had already reached his car, so it was stuffy and hot inside and smelled unmistakably of dog. He opened both doors, and while he waited for it to air out, took the floor mat out of the passenger side and gave it a good shake. When he went to put it back, he noticed a piece of paper half-under the seat. Thinking it was trash, he pulled it out. He glanced at it and his hand went instantly

to his jacket pocket. No, the flyer he'd picked up in the
street was still there. The one he held in his hand was a duplicate. And there was only one way it could have gotten
inside his car.

Sunny had to have left it there.

Rankin straightened, frowning, and looked at his watch.
Still a good fifteen or twenty minutes before Ann would be
at work. He might catch her at home, but she'd be rushed,
trying to get ready, might even be en route....

He slammed the car door. What was he thinking of,
anyway? It was none of his damn business. These people
had had their problems before he came along, and they'd
still have them after he left. He wasn't going to get involved.

But he was already involved. He'd become involved last
night, the moment he'd put his foot on the brakes and
pulled off the highway to pick up a hitchhiking teenager
and her arthritic dog. Too late, Rankin.

That was different, he told himself as he strode past the
motel office and out onto the sidewalk, head down, hands
jammed in his pockets. The child had been in danger. He'd
had no choice but to stop.

But what if the child were in danger now? What were his
choices then?

Still muttering to himself, Rankin turned the corner past
the Buckhorn Café and immediately found himself in a
residential neighborhood that looked a lot like Ann and
Sunny Severn's. The houses were old and small, surrounded by trees and flowering shrubs and tidy fences that
ought to have made them seem closed and unfriendly, but
somehow had the opposite effect. It was quiet; the growl of
a truck out on the highway seemed far away. Rankin heard
piano music coming from one house, and chickens cluck-
ing in the backyard of another. He watched two cars come
down the street from different directions and suddenly stop
when they were opposite each other. Windows were rolled
down and a conversation was struck up there in the middle
of the street. Rankin heard bits and pieces of it, along with

some laughter. Someone passing by on the other side of the street waved at him. He recognized one of the breakfast crowd from the Buckhorn and waved back.

Nice people, he thought. Nice town.

I don't belong here. I don't belong anywhere.

He looked at his watch. The bank would be opening soon.

"Annie? Are you busy?"

Ann grimaced and covered the telephone's mouthpiece with her hand. It was one of the new tellers, undoubtedly with yet another question. "I'm trying to get the loan supervisor at the Bishop office and they've got me on hold," she said with a sigh. "What can I help you with, Doreen?"

"There's a guy who wants to talk to you. He handed me this note on a deposit slip." She rolled her eyes and gave a nervous shudder. "Geez, for a minute I thought he was going to hold me up or something. He looks kind of dangerous." Her voice dropped to a whisper. "But he's *gorgeous,* too. I wonder if he's somebody famous."

Ann laughed and said, "Oh, Doreen..." as she unfolded the deposit slip with one finger. Then she hung up on the loan supervisor in the Bishop office.

"Thank you, Doreen," she said calmly, and stood up, tugging and tucking the navy-blue gabardine skirt and rose-pink blouse that were part of her color-coordinated mix-and-match working wardrobe. "I'll take care of it."

She walked up to the teller's window, steady as a rock in plain black pumps that added nearly three inches to her height, and, she felt, at least a little dignity and authority to her demeanor. In a cool, businesslike voice she said, "Good morning, Mr. Rankin. I'm surprised to see you. I thought you were going on to Los Angeles last night."

"So did I." His tone was dry. Ann found herself searching his face for the smile that had warmed and reassured her last night; without it he seemed cold, forbidding.

"Your note said—" She held it up, found to her dismay that her hand was unsteady and thrust it quickly beneath the counter. "Your note says you want to talk to me about Sunny. What is it? Is something—"

He cut her off with a gesture. "I'd rather not discuss your daughter through a window. Is there someplace perhaps a bit more private?"

Ann hesitated, then said, "Of course. Please go around to the gate and I'll buzz you in." She turned and walked away from the teller's station, her step much less confident than before. The sudden leap she'd felt beneath her ribs when she'd seen him standing there, solid and real, after he'd prowled all night through her dreams like a silver-gray intruder—the unexplainable rush of *happiness*—had settled instead into a cold, hard lump in her stomach.

She pressed the release button and held the gate for her visitor, then led the way to her desk, knowing they were drawing interested stares from her co-workers along the way.

"Please—have a seat," she said. Taking her own, she clasped her hands together on her desk blotter, like a school principal preparing to lecture a misbehaving student. Only she knew that it was to keep them from shaking. She took a deep breath, briefly closed her eyes and said, "All right, tell me, please. What has she done now? Is she all right? Did she try to...run away again?"

"That I don't know." The man's voice was brusque, business-like, so different from the way he'd been the night before. He took a piece of paper out of his jacket pocket, unfolded it and spread it on the blotter in front of her. "Have you seen this? Or anything similar to it?"

Ann scanned the paper and glanced up, puzzled. "Isn't this those religious people from up in the mountains? I don't understand. What does this have to do with Sunny?"

"Your daughter left it in my car."

"Oh," Ann said. "Well, I suppose she must have picked it up somewhere...."

"Has she mentioned anything about it to you? Expressed an interest in these people?"

"No, not really. I told you, Sunny doesn't confide in me much these days. It's her age, I guess, part of being an adolescent. But I certainly don't think there's anything wrong with it. I don't have any strong religious convictions, really, and I've tried to raise Sunny to have an open mind about other people's beliefs, and anyway, I've seen some of the kids from the camp, and they seem very nice. Very clean-cut and well-mannered. I certainly don't think they're anything to worry about. This is just a piece of paper, what can it—"

"Ann..."

There was something in the way he said her name—or maybe it was just *because* he said her name, letting her hear it spoken for the first time in his softly mysterious accent—that made her heart beat faster. She stopped talking and waited, feeling vaguely upset, frightened for no good reason.

"Ann, I've reason to believe this isn't as harmless as it looks." He hadn't taken the chair she'd offered him; she wondered if he'd chosen to stand on purpose, meaning to overwhelm her with sheer size and commanding presence. If he had, he'd miscalculated, because it made her feel more annoyed than intimidated.

"Thank you for bringing this to my attention," she said with frost in her voice. "But my daughter is my concern. Now if you—" She started to rise.

"Listen to me, please." He leaned across the desk and covered her hand with his. She stared down at his scarred, battered hand and felt her anger evaporate and a confusion of emotions take its place. "I've seen more of this kind of thing than you can possibly imagine." His voice was soft but intense. "It's pure propaganda, and it's aimed at kids like your daughter. This is just the first step, meant to catch her interest. Next they'll begin to recruit her in earnest, and they will know exactly how to play on her vulnerabilities. They will make her feel special, important. Meanwhile, they'll be cutting her out of the herd, making her feel isolated, alienated from everyone who cares about her. They'll make her believe that they are the only ones who care about her, the only ones who can give her what she needs, until she becomes completely dependent on them emotionally. In the end, she will do anything they tell her to do. *Anything,* do you understand? They will think for her. Like a person on drugs, she will have no conscience, no will of her own. She will be like a puppet...." He paused and let his breath out slowly. "Or a robot."

Ann had been staring at him, feeling cold and sick. "That's ridiculous," she said flatly. "I don't believe it."

"Believe it." His hand tightened, his voice roughened. "Think about it—extreme cases make the headlines. You've heard of Hitler Youth, Jonestown, Charles Manson—"

Appalled, Ann pulled her hand away from him. "Now, that really *is* ridiculous," she said testily, not wanting to let him see he'd frightened her. "These people aren't criminals, they're a religious group. I appreciate your concern, but I really don't think Sunny would be interested in anything like that. She doesn't even like to go to Sunday School anymore. No, really, Mr. Rankin, thank you for bringing it to my attention, but I'm sure there's nothing to worry about."

For a long moment he stayed where he was, leaning on his hands, his eyes on a level with hers, eyes a clear sharp blue that seemed to see inside her. And for that moment she felt panic. She was sure he could hear the jackhammer pounding of her heart, see the cold sweat on her palms, feel the dryness in her throat. She was certain he knew her deepest, blackest fear, the fear that had dogged her for over twelve years, the fear that haunted her nightmares and every waking moment. The fear that, in spite of everything she tried to do, she was going to lose her daughter. The fear that Sunny was slipping away from her, too, just as Mark had, and there wasn't anything she could do to stop it.

He knows, she thought suddenly. Somehow, this big man with the cold eyes, elegant bearing and battered hands knows how it is to feel frightened and helpless, and not in control.

As she watched them, the blue eyes seemed to soften. A smile appeared. It was a wry smile, without the charm she remembered, but a smile nonetheless. The man straightened and said, "All right, then. It's your business. I just thought you should know. Thanks for your time."

He turned to go, and with every step he took Ann felt as if she were coming unraveled. All of a sudden she wanted to run after him. She wanted to cling to those strong, ravaged hands and tell him how frightened she was, tell him that she needed help, that something was terribly wrong with her child and she didn't know how to fix it.

"Mr. Rankin. Neal—"

He looked back at her, one eyebrow raised in unspoken query.

She came around her desk, picking up a pencil on the way and toying with it to hide her nervousness. "I really do want to thank you—for everything. For last night, and uh..." Several interested faces were turning their way. Ann coughed and moved closer to him, lowering her voice to a murmur. "And for... for caring."

"Don't mention it."

Ann moved past him to the security gate, but instead of pressing the release button, rested her hands on top of it and stared at them as she said, "So, I guess you'll be on your way now... to Los Angeles?"

"No," the man named Rankin said. "I've had a change of plans."

"Oh." Her heart was racing. She looked up quickly and caught an odd expression on his face, one she couldn't read at all. "You have?"

"Yes. I think I'm going to be staying on for a day or two."

Ann's heartbeat stumbled, then righted itself. "Oh," she said, "that's nice." She opened the gate and held it for him, then followed him through it, somehow unable to bear the thought of closing herself off from him. Not yet, she told herself. Not yet . . .

She walked beside him to the front door, conscious of the fact that, in her high heels, at least, her head actually topped his shoulder. Her mind was reeling, her insides quivering. She knew that all the people she worked with, not to mention several familiar customers, were watching her, wondering about her, all but eaten alive with curiosity about her mysterious visitor in the elegant clothes. And she didn't care.

At the door she paused and took a deep breath. Her heart was trying to batter a hole in her chest. "Mr. Rankin—"

"It was Neal a moment ago," he said with his little half smile.

"Neal . . . I was wondering, since you're going to be staying in town, I thought, if you're tired of restaurant cooking . . . it wouldn't be anything fancy, but I thought you'd like to come and have dinner with Sunny and me. It's the least I can do, to thank you for being so kind. God knows where Sunny might be right now if you hadn't come along when you did, and it might be a nice change for you, after—"

"Thank you. I'd like to come."

"You would?" It was an airless whisper; her breath had all been taken up by that particular explosion of joy and panic she hadn't felt since she was a teenager. "Is tonight all right? Around . . . seven? Or you could come earlier if you want. We're pretty informal, just—"

"Seven is fine. I'll be there." He gave her a smile, the one she'd been waiting for, and slipped through the door.

Ann collapsed against it, then instantly straightened and inquired of a dozen or so pairs of avid eyes, "Well, what are *you* looking at?"

Why did I say that? Rankin wondered as he stood on the sidewalk in front of the Sierra National Bank, waiting for his eyes to adjust to the glare. When had he decided to stay in this truck-stop town on the edge of nowhere? When had he decided to make these people's business *his* business?

But he knew when. He knew exactly when. He'd made up his mind the moment he'd seen the look of fear in Ann Severn's brown eyes. Oh, she'd tried to hide it from him, acting so cool and unconcerned. But he was good at reading people, adept at seeing beyond the defenses and facades they erected to hide their feelings. He'd had to be in order to survive. And he knew that, for all her apparent coldness, Ann was scared to death about her daughter. He wanted to know why.

A cream-colored sedan was parked at the curb. Bill Clemson leaned against the front fender, arms folded across his chest, long legs crossed at the ankles. When he saw Rankin he touched a forefinger to his aviator sunglasses and said in a friendly way, "Doing a little banking?"

"Something like that," Rankin said as he strolled over to the car. "You get that report you were waiting for?"

"Yep, I got it." The sheriff straightened up slowly, almost lazily, and opened the door on the passenger's side. "Where you headed? I'll give you a lift."

Rankin raised an eyebrow. "Is this a service you provide all your visitors, or was there something interesting in that report after all?"

"What?" Bill said with bland innocence. "Aw, hell no, this is just a friendly gesture."

"In that case," said Rankin, "you can drop me at the Whispering Pines Motel." He ducked his head and settled into the passenger's seat. Bill shut the door on him and went around to the driver's side.

"You can clear up one thing for me, though," he said as he eased in behind the wheel. He took the small piece of paper out of his uniform pocket again, glanced at it and handed it to Rankin. "How the hell do you pronounce your name? N-i-a-l-l... what is that, anyway?"

"My mother pronounced it Neal," Rankin said. "But she was German. I believe the name is Gaelic."

"Ah," Bill said. And after a brief pause, "So you're from Germany, are you?"

"I was born there, yes. West Berlin."

"Rankin . . . that's not a German name."

"No," Rankin said easily, "my father was Irish-American—a G.I., as a matter of fact." A cynical smile quirked the corners of his mouth; he would have been amused by the sheriff's questions, if he hadn't been certain there was serious intent behind them. He wanted something from him; Rankin knew that the same way he'd known the sheriff's visit to the Buckhorn that morning had been for the express purpose of seeking him out. Now, as then, he didn't ask questions of his own. He was a patient man.

"No kiddin', a G.I.?" The sheriff turned on his radio and picked up the hand unit. "Nancy, this is Bill. What have you got for me?"

The dispatcher's voice came through the usual static. "Not a thing, Bill. Pretty quiet. Fred's back from Bishop—he's doing the paperwork on that vandalism at the Boron plant. Ramon just called in from out on 136—"

"Okay, Nancy, I'm going off duty for a couple hours. Anything comes up, you give me a holler." He hung up the unit and sat back, drumming his fingers on the steering wheel and whistling soundlessly through his teeth. Rankin waited. After a moment or two the sheriff took off his sunglasses and tossed them on the dashboard. "Dammit, Rankin," he said, shaking his head, "I have to tell you, I've got a problem with you."

"Sorry to hear that," Rankin said sympathetically.

The sheriff gave him a sideways look. "See, I'm pretty good at putting two and two together. I can usually tell when they don't add up to four, know what I mean?" He shifted suddenly so he was facing Rankin, his gaze hard and direct. "Now, if I'm to believe that report, you have got to be just about the dullest, damn bureaucrat in Washington. Never saw such a clean record—not even a parking ticket."

Rankin chuckled. "Sorry to disappoint you. I live a very uninteresting life."

"Yeah, I mighta bought that," Bill said. "Before I had breakfast with you and got a good look at you. Especially your hands." He paused and then said softly, "Mr. Rankin, your record says you're clean. But somewhere, sometime, those hands of yours tell me you've done hard time."

Four

"I knew a guy once," the sheriff went on, still speaking softly, almost musingly. "It was in the academy. This guy had been a POW in Nam. Had a pretty rough time of it, I guess. Some torture...did time in those tiger cages, spent a lot of time with his hands tied, know what I mean? Now, he had scars like yours—only other time in my life I've ever seen scars like that."

He paused, but Rankin didn't say anything. He was wishing to God he had a cigarette.

Bill squinted thoughtfully. "I don't see you in Nam, though. Way I figure it, you got caught in a different kind of war entirely. Am I right?"

Rankin gave a noncommittal shrug. "This is your story."

"Okay, so what've we got here?" Bill continued, as if he hadn't spoken. "One, you've done time, but from the treatment those hands got, I'd lay odds it wasn't in this country. Two, in spite of that your record's clean, which means it's been laundered. And by somebody who knows how to do the job right. Now what that says to me is, there's more to this Niall Rankin than meets the eye. See what I mean? I'm adding things up, here." He studied Rankin with half-closed eyes. "I don't see you as the three-piece, gray-flannel suit type, so I'd make you...CIA. Or maybe something even farther underground. One of those top-secret Cold War agencies everybody always denies the existence of." And then, without missing a beat he fired point blank: "Where'd you get those scars—Russia?"

"No," Rankin countered, just as matter-of-factly. "East Berlin."

"Yeah?" The expression on Bill's face was pure curiosity, without a hint of self-congratulation. "How long?"

"Five years."

The sheriff gave a soundless whistle. "That's a long time."

"Ancient history," Rankin said, his voice remote. "I was very young...." He paused. "And foolish."

"What did you do that got you locked up in an East German prison for five years?"

Rankin smiled a thin, cold smile, and didn't tell him that compared to the places he'd spent most of those five years, prison would have seemed like paradise. "I was helping people escape," he said. "Through—actually under—the Wall."

"Tunnel?"

"That's right. We'd taken two groups through. We were getting ready to take the third. The secret police surprised us at the rendezvous point."

"Tough luck."

"Luck had nothing to do with it. One of our group betrayed us." He said the words in a flat, cold voice, insulating himself beneath layers and layers of ice, the way he always did when he thought of Marta. He flexed the fingers of his right hand, remembering the times he'd imagined them curled around her throat...the soft white throat he'd so often caressed...marked with his love bites. He laughed, knowing it wasn't a pleasant sound. "They gave me these because they thought it would encourage me to tell them where the tunnel was.''

"Did it?"

"No."

Bill Clemson let his breath out slowly. He put on his sunglasses and was reaching for the ignition when Rankin said bluntly, "Why this avid interest in me and my business, past and present? Like I told you, I'm just a traveler, passing through. I'm no threat, either to you, or...anyone else in your town."

"Actually," Bill said, giving him a quick glance as he pulled away from the curb, "I never did think of you as a ... *threat,* exactly." He faced front again, squinting behind his sunglasses. "What I was kind of hoping was, you might be able to help me out."

Rankin's eyebrows went up in surprise, and he wasn't easily surprised. But he only said mildly, "I can't imagine what I might be in a position to help you with."

Bill shifted restlessly in his seat, then looked over at Rankin and laughed. "Like hell you can't. Mr. Rankin, I have a feeling you know damn good and well what I want from you."

Rankin didn't say anything. The sheriff made a soft, frustrated sound and looked away, out the window, across the lava-strewn foothills to where the Sierra Nevadas rose in stark relief against a brilliant sky.

"Rankin, let me tell you something. Those people up there in that compound bother me. I can't tell you why— call it instinct, which is something I have a feeling you know about. Officially, I can't touch 'em. If I get within a mile of the place without a damn good reason, they'll have me for harassment, violation of the First Amendment rights—you name it. And they're making sure they don't give me a reason. No...what I need is somebody to get inside that place for me. Take a look around. A little *unofficial* visit, you follow me?"

He paused, measuring Rankin with his eyes. Assessing him, gauging his response. Then he said very softly, "And that, Mr. Rankin, is something else I think maybe you know about.''

It was silent in the car, except for the wind and engine sounds and an occasional rustle of static from the radio. They were heading north, the highway arrow-straight at that point but rising steadily, undulating gently over brush-dotted hills. Up ahead the Sierra escarpment loomed in varying shades of blue and purple and indigo. Rankin watched a coyote lope unhurriedly across the road in front of them, reminding him of the event that had brought him to this place, and said, ''Sheriff, I have only one question.''

The sheriff glanced over at him. ''Shoot.''

''Why me? Of all the people who must pass through your town, what made you decide I'm your man?''

Bill gave him another look and asked pointedly, ''Are you?''

''Answer my question,'' Rankin said, ''and I'll tell you.''

''Aw, hell,'' Bill muttered, his sunburn flaring, ''if I tell you, you'll probably think I'm as crazy as those people up there in the hills. Don't get me wrong. I'm a church-goin' man—go with my wife and kids every Sunday I can—but it's kind of like a habit, if you know what I mean. Never did believe in the notion there was Somebody watching everything I did and pulling strings. But every now and then something happens that kind of makes you wonder, you know? About things like Fate...Providence...*you* know....

''See, the way it happened was this, Annie was talking to me on the phone when she saw you drive up with Sunny. And she hung up on me. I was curious—hell, I was worried about her—so I thought I'd drive over and check things out, just to be on the safe side.'' He threw Rankin another look, and a little half-smile. ''While you were inside with Annie, I ran a make on your car.''

''Ah,'' murmured Rankin. ''I wondered.''

''Anyway, when it came up a rental, with those Virginia plates, I got to thinking about that, and the more I thought about it, the more it seemed like a strange thing for a man to do—drive all alone from coast to coast and back again. Either that or those drop-off charges are going to kill you. So I called up a P.I. I know in Washington—got him out of bed, I'm going to owe him one hell of a favor—and told him to get me anything he could find on a man named Niall Rankin. The rest you know. I just started adding two and two."

Rankin was silent. He was having a vision of himself lighting up a cigarette, hearing the faint crackle of burning paper, smelling the aroma of tobacco, feeling the burn of that first drag all the way down to his belly....

"Plus, there's one more thing."

"What's that?" Rankin asked, exhaling slowly.

"Mr. Rankin, we live in a world where people close their windows so they won't have to listen to a cry for help." Bill's voice was very soft. "You picked up that kid in the middle of nowhere and brought her home to her mother, and you went miles out of your way and lost time doing it. That tells me a lot of what I need to know about you."

"And the rest?"

"Like I said, I just add up two and two." The sheriff shook his head. "Rankin, I've been in this business a long time. I know a man on the run when I see one. Now, I don't know what from, or where you're going, and the way I figure it, maybe you don't either. I figure you just might have a day or two that isn't going to cost you one way or the other."

Rankin kept his eyes on the window and watched the changing terrain go by. The road was winding now, climbing rapidly; in a few more turns they'd be in timber.

"Well, what about it?" the sheriff asked after a few minutes of the silence, a tiny muscle tugging at the corner of his mouth. "Feel like staying around for a couple of days? Maybe do a little...backpacking?"

"I guess my business in Los Angeles can wait a day or two," Rankin said slowly, thoughtfully. He turned to Bill with a smile. "God knows, I could use the exercise. I'm pretty out of shape. They put me behind a desk a while back—something I've never been able to get used to.''

Bill Clemson grinned and slapped the steering wheel with his hand in exultation. "Rankin, I can't tell you how happy it makes me to hear that. The staying, I mean." He threw Rankin a measuring look. "Can't quite see you as a desk jockey," he said.

"Neither can I," Rankin said dryly, and decided not to tell him he'd made the decision to stay a few more days in Pinetree before he'd even set foot in the sheriff's car. He couldn't help but think, though, how strangely things turned out, sometimes. It was almost enough to make *him* believe in Fate . . . or Providence.

"I don't see why I have to be here," Sunny said, looking mutinous.

"Oh, honey, come on, now. It's been a long time since we've had company for dinner." Ann made her tone light, striving for patience. The last thing she wanted, tonight of all nights, was a fight with Sunny. "I just thought it would be nice. . . ." She picked up a pot holder and took another look at the roast that was browning in the oven. "It will give you a chance to say thank you."

"For what?"

"For giving you a ride home last night. It was nice of him. That's why I invited him—to say thank you."

"Yeah, *right*." Sunny made a rude noise as she pushed through the kitchen door.

"Sunny—" Ann thought about calling her back, then put down the pot holder and went after her instead, taking a deep calming breath. It's just nerves, she told herself; it's been so long since I fixed dinner for company.

Not for company—for a man. And not just a man—for *this* man. She wanted everything to go right. To be perfect. She wanted, just once in her life, to be polished and elegant and sophisticated, like he was.

At her daughter's bedroom door she hesitated, then knocked and pushed it open. "Sunny? I forgot to tell you, Will called."

Sunny was lying on her stomach across her unmade bed, picking at the stitching on one of Grandma's comforters. She didn't look up. "Yeah, so what?"

"He wants you to call him back. He said he's been trying to reach you since yesterday." Sunny kept sullenly silent. Ann sat down on the bed beside her. She reached out a hand to stroke the hair out of her daughter's face but pulled it back without touching her as she said in a cajoling tone, "Honey, why don't you call him? I think it might be about the dance...." Sunny snorted and went on picking at the quilt. "Well, why not? I thought that was what you wanted. You've always had a . . . well, kind of a crush on Will—"

"Will Clemson is a *jerk,*" Sunny said as she bounced up off the bed. "I *hate* him. And I wouldn't go to that stupid dance if you *paid* me!" The last word was cut off by the bedroom door. A moment later the front door slammed, shaking the house.

Ann sat where she was for a few minutes, swallowing her anger along with a cold, lonely feeling of futility. Then she got up and went back to the kitchen.

The girl—Sunny—was sitting on the front steps in the semidarkness when he walked through the gate. The old black dog was asleep in the soft dirt near her feet, pretty much where he'd left him the night before. Neither one moved as he came up the walk, although Sunny, at least, acknowledged Rankin's presence with a long, sullen glare. He'd had friendlier receptions from the KGB.

"Sunshine. Nice to see you again," he said pleasantly, giving her a sardonic little bow.

"Do go in," she replied with withering sarcasm of her own. "My mother is in the kitchen, preparing the fatted calf."

"Oh really?" Rankin arched an eyebrow at the choice of phrases, wondering if its biblical origin was coincidence. "Then I guess it's a good thing I brought red wine."

"Wine." Sunny snorted. "That's perfect. Mom doesn't drink it."

"That's all right, I do," said Rankin cheerfully as he went up the steps, pausing to drop a box into her lap. "Here, this is for you."

"Candy," Sunny muttered. "Gee, thanks, I'm on a diet."

Rankin laughed softly and stepped around her. With his peripheral vision he saw her cast him one furtive glance, then pick up the box of chocolate mint wafers. He went into the house, chuckling and shaking his head. Pretty girl, he thought. Looked a lot like her mother. And with a disposition like Attila the Hun's. He wondered what it was that had her so angry...so alienated...so lonely. He wondered why he liked her so much. He wondered why he was beginning to care what happened to her. To worry about her.

And then her mother came out of the kitchen, wiping her hands on a dish towel, and he thought he knew at least one reason.

He hadn't known until that moment just how much he'd been looking forward to seeing Ann Severn again. She was wearing a pink dress made out of sweater material, with long sleeves and a V neck, so soft-looking it made his fingers itch with the urge to touch it. But he'd discovered this morning at the bank that Ann's particular softness had very little to do with what she wore, or how she fixed her hair. She'd been wearing a suit then, just like the one he'd tried to imagine her in, and her hair had been pulled back in some sort of bun. He smiled at the memory, wondering if she'd had any idea how that deep rose color had bathed her skin, making her look as if she'd just been kissed, or that the slippery-clean strands of hair slipping out of the bun and down her neck made a man think about pulling the rest of it free and burying his hands and face in it. He wondered if she knew, right now, at this moment, how that dress she was wearing molded, defined and praised every feminine curve and wrapped it all in voluptuous softness that seemed to promise both solace and delight. Something about the way she moved in it, and the shy way she smiled made him doubt it; she had a body to haunt a man's dreams, and the face of a five-year-old with a handful of crumpled daisies hidden behind her back.

But then, with women as with men, Rankin had learned the hard way not to trust appearances. And it was his experience that no woman past the age of five was ever completely unaware of her own sex appeal.

So, she's dressed up for me, he thought as he smiled down at her. He wondered why that didn't make him feel edgy and cynical.

"Hi," she said, pushing at stray wisps of hair with the back of her hand. She looked heat-flushed and breathless.

"Sunny suggested I come on in," said Rankin. "I hope you don't mind." He handed her the bottle of wine and added dryly, "She also tells me you don't drink. Perhaps I should have brought flowers."

A series of emotions flitted across her face, too fast for him to catch. Surprise, consternation, and a certain wistfulness were only a few. "Well, Sunny doesn't know everything. She only thinks she does," she said lightly. "It was thoughtful of you, Mr. Rankin—"

Rankin's eyebrow rose. "It's back to that again, is it?"

"I beg your pardon?"

"It was Niall this morning."

"Well, yeah, I was pretty sure it was," she said, looking uncertain, "but then I was noticing that note you left me, and . . . you spell it differently, don't you?"

Rankin nodded and spelled it again for her. She pronounced it, giving it a flatter, more domesticated sound that rather intrigued him. He seldom used his first name, having tired long ago of explaining it to strangers, but he decided he liked the way Ann said it.

"Anyway," she went on with a smile, "you really didn't need to bring anything—except yourself, of course."

"A custom I grew up with," Rankin said dismissively, moving past her, into the kitchen. It was as warm as he remembered—too warm. He went on through and opened the back door, drawing in a deep breath of cold evening air.

Yes, he thought, definitely lilacs.

"That was in . . . Germany?" Ann asked, following him.

"Yes." He moved over, making room for her in the open doorway, smiling down at her as he did. "I hope you don't mind. The fresh air feels good, doesn't it? Is that lilacs I smell?"

"Mmm, I guess it is," she murmured, sniffing judiciously. "I don't really notice it. I guess I take it for granted." She looked up at him. "Do you like the smell of lilacs? I always associate them with my childhood, for some reason. They remind me of my grandmother, I guess because there were huge bushes in her yard—armloads and armloads of lilacs, usually just in time for Easter." She folded her arms across herself in a spontaneous little hug. "I love spring, don't you? It's my favorite time of year. Everything starts all over again, fresh and clean and new."

She took a deep breath and so did Rankin. He pulled the clean air deep into his lungs and was glad for once that he'd finally managed to quit smoking. He didn't tell her, of course, that there had been no lilacs in his childhood, that his earliest playgrounds had been bombed-out ruins and rubble-strewn lots. He wondered, though, whether it was true, what she'd said about spring, and whether it would ever be possible for him to start over again . . . fresh and clean and new.

The panther in the barnyard . . . The image was there in Ann's mind as she stood beside him, seeing the glitter of something cold and lonely come and go in his eyes.

But who is this man? she wondered. What can his world be like, that he feels so lost in mine?

She felt a great wave of sadness, because, like the ghost-panther of her childhood, he would walk only briefly through her world and then vanish without a trace. And like the panther, she would never, ever forget him.

"I'll go and call Sunny," she said, stepping back into her warm kitchen, away from the darkness and the cold outside, and the disturbingly irresistible presence in the doorway. "The roast is almost done. Can I...get you anything? Something to drink?"

"No, thank you," Niall said. "Can I help you with anything?"

Ann assured him politely that everything had been taken care of, that he had only to relax and enjoy himself. But she was thinking in sudden despair how awkward it all was, and what a stupid idea it had been to invite him here. What could she have been thinking of? She didn't know this man at all, and she'd never been comfortable with strangers.

"I know," she said brightly, "you can open the wine. Only I'm not sure if I have a corkscrew." What must he think of her? She didn't know how to be anything other than what she was, which was small-town, down-home simple. Most of the men she knew drank beer, and she rarely drank anything at all. Why would she have a corkscrew?

"It's all right," he said. "I do." He smiled at her—the charming smile that changed his eyes—and took a folding knife out of his pocket, one of the ones with all sorts of gadgets whose uses she could only guess. Mark had had one similar to it when he came back from Vietnam, she remembered, but she'd never seen one as complex as this one. It seemed an odd thing for a man of such elegance to carry, but it did look at home in those hard-weathered hands.

She lingered for a moment, watching him, watching his hands as they carefully manipulated the bottle and corkscrew. The awkwardness and panic she'd felt a moment ago dissipated and an odd, hot quivering took its place. It had been a long time since she'd felt anything like that.

Like someone escaping from quicksand, she tore herself away and went to find Sunny.

They ate in the living room, at the big table by the window, on one of Grandma's white tablecloths, a fact that Sunny had noted and made several sarcastic comments about. Ann couldn't understand it. Not the sarcasm, which seemed to have become her daughter's principal mode of communication lately, but her attitude toward Niall Rankin. When Ann had started dating again, about two years after Mark's death, it had been due more to Sunny's wistful and highly vocal longing for "a new daddy" rather than any real desire on Ann's part for male companionship. And while in the last few years Sunny's interest in Ann's sporadic dates had dwindled to mild indifference, this rudeness and open hostility were new.

All through dinner Sunny sat hunched over her plate, stabbing at her food and generally casting an uneasy pall over what Ann thought was a pretty nice effort, considering how little real cooking she did these days. The roast was rare in the middle and well-done on the outside, so if someone didn't like it one way they could have it the other; the vegetables were frozen, but the potatoes were ovenbrowned, tender and flaky inside, the way her grandmother had always fixed them. At first Sunny's behavior embarrassed Ann and filled her with a strong urge to kick her daughter under the table, but after awhile she forgot about it; she had other things on her mind.

Niall had managed to get the wine bottle opened. Ann got out her only stemware, the two champagne glasses she'd saved from her wedding reception, and didn't object when he poured them both three-quarters full. He lifted his glass toward Ann and murmured, "Cheers." Sunny snorted, but Ann lifted hers, too, caught her lower lip between her teeth to hold back a little chuckle of nervousness and excitement and took a brave sip. It tasted as bad as she remembered.

Look at her, Sunny thought, eyeing her mother in disgust. It was unbelievable. Flirting, for God's sake. At her age. Didn't she know how dumb she looked? And drinking wine—she didn't even drink!

Sunny didn't understand it. What was the guy still hanging around Pinetree for, anyway? He'd been on his way to L.A. when he stopped to pick her up, she was certain of it. Why hadn't he gone on his way and just minded his own business? He sure didn't belong here; that was obvious. He stuck out like a sore thumb in this stupid town. What was her mother thinking of?

Probably just sex, she told herself cynically. Which was a really gross idea, but what else could it be? The guy sure didn't look the husband and stepfather type to her. She probably ought to be glad about that. The last thing in the world she wanted was a stepfather. All it would be was one more person bossing her around, telling her what to do. Who needed it? It had been different when she was little. All her friends had had daddies, and she'd really envied them and had tried to talk her mother into getting married so she could have one, too. Now that she was older and smarter, she was kind of glad it hadn't worked out. Who needed a father, anyway?

And if I ever did have one, she thought, stabbing wretchedly at a carrot, it wouldn't be a jerk like that. It wasn't going to be some sophisticated foreigner who looked like he'd just stepped out of a magazine ad, who wasn't about to hang out in a place like Pinetree for long anyway, and who sooner or later was going to go back where he belonged and break her mother's heart and leave her all alone again. Not Sunny, though. She wasn't going to get her heart broken, no sir. Who needed it?

"Sunny," her mother said in that syrupy voice she used all the time lately, "if you're through eating, why don't you help me clear away the dishes. We have ice cream for dessert."

"Dessert too?" cooed Sunny. "My goodness, you really did go all out, didn't you?"

Her mother's face got pink, but Sunny knew she wouldn't say anything, not with *him* here. She could feel him watching her, too, with those eyes of his that could see right inside her. For some reason, she began to feel guilty.

And since she hated feeling guilty almost more than anything in the whole world, she got angry instead.

"I don't believe I care for any dessert," she said with exaggerated courtesy. "If you will please excuse me . . . ?"

"Sunny, I'd like you to—"

"Thank you, Mummy dearest," Sunny said with her most insincere smile, pushing back her chair. "I shall be in my room."

In the silence following Sunny's exit, Ann picked up her wineglass and drained it like a thirsty child. Rankin lifted the bottle and murmured, "May I?"

"No, thank you," she said absently, then turned upon him a smile of false radiance, all teeth and desperate, shimmering eyes. "Well, would *you* care for some ice cream?"

She jumped up without waiting for his reply, groped for and clutched at the back of her chair. Then she said, "Whoa," looking startled, and sat down again. "I'm *dizzy*. Good heavens—am I *drunk?*"

Five

―――

"I don't think so," Rankin said, struggling with a smile. "Not on one glass of wine." If she was, he'd never seen anyone look cuter in that condition, with her cheeks as pink as the dress she was wearing—though he thought that was partly from embarrassment—her eyes wide and bewildered.

"I'm not used to it. I probably shouldn't have." She frowned. "My head feels funny."

"You probably just need some fresh air," Rankin suggested gently. "Would you like to go for a walk?"

She hesitated, then said, "Yes, thank you, I'd like that." Dignity recovered, she pushed her chair back and rose, more carefully this time.

Rankin watched her walk across the room to the coat closet just inside the hallway, her step steady but a little stiff, a little awkward, as if she knew his eyes were on her. He watched her open the door and take out his coat and then hers. She turned, hugging the coats to her chest, paused as if to gather courage, then knocked lightly on the door of her daughter's room.

"Sunny?" When there was no answer she turned the knob, pushed the door partly open and called through the crack. "Sunny, we're going out for a walk, to get some fresh air. I want you to clear the table while we're gone. Put the food in the refrigerator and stack the dishes in the sink. Will you do that for me, please?"

Rankin didn't hear a reply, but Ann was apparently satisfied. She came toward him, carrying the coats and wearing her too-bright smile. "Well, shall we go?"

He held her coat for her, noting a moment's surprise and hesitation, and a certain clumsiness as she groped for the armholes. It touched him unexpectedly. Without knowing quite how, he found himself with his hands full of her hair; he was lifting it off her neck while she adjusted her collar, the warm, soft weight of it pouring over his hands like melted honey. She tilted her head to look up at him, and he felt that falling-down-a-mine-shaft sensation he'd experienced in his youth, when he'd known he was about to kiss someone.

For a heartbeat or two—or maybe more, who was counting?—he thought about it. Thought about how her skin would feel against his fingertips, her lips against his. Velvet soft...nice. Maybe more than nice. The warm, sweet taste of her mouth...the hot brandy taste of passion...

He lifted his hands abruptly from her shoulders. Whoa, Rankin, what the hell do you think you're doing? He could have kissed her, he knew that beyond any doubt, and maybe that was what made it out of the question. For some reason, she seemed to be as attracted to him as he was to her, and he had an idea that if she kissed him she wouldn't hold anything back. It would be up to him to hold the line, to keep it from going beyond a kiss, and he wasn't sure he could do that. It had been a long time since he'd kissed a woman, and even longer since he'd thought about one the way he was thinking about Ann right now.

Just for a moment he wished she were someone else, a different kind of woman, one who knew the rules of the game and understood that he had nothing at all to give her beyond that temporary gratification. Someone who would take what he did have to offer and give him back the same, with no strings attached. Then, he thought, then he might take all he could of her sweet, soft mouth, gladly immerse himself in her warm, silken body and forget that while her life was here in this oasis, his was in limbo, and that in two or three days he was going to go away and leave this place, and her, and most likely never see either of them again.

But she wasn't someone else. And kissing her was out of the question.

"I'm sorry," Ann said as they went down the front walk.

Rankin opened the gate and held it for her. "Sorry? For what?"

He heard her sigh. "Oh, for Sunny. For her behavior. She really was awful tonight. I don't know what gets into her sometimes." She glanced quickly at Rankin, then away, and said lightly, glibly, "Oh, I'm sure it's just her age. It's so hard for kids now, growing up, I mean. Harder than when I was her age. The world is changing so fast, don't you think? It's so much more complicated now."

"It's changing," Rankin said dryly. "I'm not sure it's more complicated, but it certainly is changing."

He felt her look at him but she didn't say anything more, and they walked a ways in silence.

Ann was wearing high heels, which she seemed comfortable enough in, but outside the gate there were no sidewalks and the ground was uneven, so she had to go carefully, picking her way. Once she stumbled, and when she reached reflexively to steady herself with a hand on his arm, Rankin caught her fingers and tucked them in the bend of his elbow.

"Your hand is cold," he remarked softly, covering it with his.

She laughed and murmured, "Yours is warm."

There were no street lights; what light there was came from the stars, or spilled from the windows and front porches of the houses they passed. A dog barked, interrupting a burst of canned laughter from someone's TV set; a car loaded with teenagers passed by on a cross street, stereo speakers thumping; out on the highway a truck snarled as it down-shifted for the caution light. A cold, dry desert breeze crept inside the neck of Rankin's jacket, making him restless and edgy.

He hunched his shoulders against the chill and said abruptly, "Did you ever think about leaving this place?"

She looked at him, startled. "Leave Pinetree? Why?"

He didn't answer her right away, but reached automatically for his cigarettes instead. Remembering, he made an impatient gesture with the hand and said, "I met a friend of yours today—Bill Clemson. He told me how your husband died."

"Oh," Ann said. "I see." Rankin felt tension in her fingers and tightened his just in time to keep her from pulling away.

"It must have been hard for you," he persisted gently. "Hard for Sunny, too."

"Not really." Her voice had become remote. "Sunny was hardly more than a baby then. Too young to understand."

"*Then.* What about later, when she got older?" He paused. "What about now?" She didn't reply, just walked beside him, her eyes on the ground ahead of her. After another pause Rankin said, "Do people still talk about it?"

She shrugged. "I don't know, not to me." Her words were cool and unconcerned, but Rankin noticed that her fingers felt stiff and cold even in the warmth of his hand.

"It just seems to me," he said casually, "that it might have been better—for you, and for Sunny—to have moved away from here. To have started somewhere else, fresh, without all the..." He hesitated, then finished with dissatisfaction, "Memories." He knew only too well that memories weren't so easily evaded.

She laughed and lifted her head; the gremlin wind that Rankin found so discomfiting made gentle mischief with her hair, like a playful sprite. "But this is my home," she said simply. "This is where I was born. These people are my friends, my family. I belong here."

Rankin, struggling to understand, didn't reply.

"I guess some people might not understand that," she went on with a touch of sadness. They walked in silence while she searched for the words to explain. After a while she laughed again, softly. "My grandpa always said there are two kinds of people, pioneers and settlers, and that the world needs both kinds, otherwise we'd still be living in trees. He always said he was a settler—then he'd wink and say he'd had to be, otherwise Grandma never would have married him.

"My dad, though—Daddy was definitely a pioneer, or anyway, a wanderer. He was a professional rodeo cowboy. Mom met him while she was still in high school, at a dance in Carson City. She followed him around the circuit for years, even though I think she was a settler herself, at heart. It was all right while it was just the two of them, I guess, but when she knew I was on the way, she insisted they were going to settle down. She'd lost a baby—a boy—before I was born, and maybe she didn't want to take any chances with me. So they bought a store—feed and tack, Western wear, things like that—here in Pinetree." She waited a moment, then shrugged as if to say, And here I am....

But Rankin wasn't satisfied with that. "And how did it work out?" he persisted, his voice unexpectedly harsh.

"What do you mean?"

"Were they... happy, all settled down here in Pinetree, California?"

Once again he heard her sigh. "I think Mom was, but Daddy never could get rodeoing out of his system. He tried, but I guess he just needed that excitement... the danger. Eventually he went back to following the circuit, so I never saw very much of him while I was little. And then when I was nine he got broken up pretty bad—it was a roping accident, he'd given up bronc riding by then—and while he was recuperating from that he got pneumonia and died. So I guess you could say he never did settle down."

"And your mother? Does she still live here?"

She shook her head; he felt her hair brush against his shoulders. "No. After Daddy died, Mom ran the feed store until she got too sick and had to sell it. She died when Sunny was a baby. Lung cancer."

Rankin, who had been longing for a cigarette, coughed and murmured, "I'm sorry." After a moment he said reflectively, "You've had a great many losses in your life."

She looked at him and then away. "Everyone has losses. It's part of life. You can let them beat you down, or you can get up and get on with your life." He felt her shrug again. "It's that simple."

Walking beside her in the darkness, with her hair blowing soft against his shoulder and her hand curled like a sleeping bird in his, Rankin thought of Bill Clemson's words: *Annie's tougher than she looks.* And maybe because of the darkness that kept him from seeing her softness, he felt in her what he'd missed before—the strength, the resilience, the courage. Once more proving, he thought wryly, the folly of making judgments based on appearances. The lady was about as soft as tempered steel.

But, he reminded himself, even steel has its breaking point. He wondered what Ann's would be. Sunny? Oh yeah, he thought, a woman might lose both parents and a husband and fight her way back, but how would she bear the loss of her only child? Suddenly he was remembering the fear in her eyes when he'd told her about the leaflet he'd found in his car; the way she'd flinched when he'd suggested Sunny might have been running away from home; the way she'd had to fortify herself before knocking on her daughter's bedroom door, as if she were facing a den of lions. Losing Sunny—*that's* what she's afraid of, he thought. So afraid she's paralyzed . . .

"It's easier," Ann said, looking up at him, "when you have people around you—family, friends—who know you and care about you. I guess that's why I've stayed in Pine-tree.''

She let go of his arm long enough to break a sprig of flowers from a bush overhanging a fence they were pass-ing. ''Mrs. Jensen won't mind,'' she murmured, handing the leafy spray to Rankin. ''There. Now you can make a memory.''

He lifted the blossoms to his face and inhaled the sweet scent of lilacs. Cradling the fat, fragile cluster of tiny flowers in his hand, he asked softly, ''And how do you 'make a memory'?''

''Smells make memories, don't you know that? I told you that every time I smell lilacs I think of my grand-mother, and my grandparents' place.'' She laughed, a light, breathless sound. ''Maybe... maybe now, every time you smell lilacs you'll think of Pinetree... and me.''

I'll think of you, don't worry. He caught her hand in an impulsive gesture and they walked on, hands clasped, in a silent companionship that was entirely new to him. He didn't say anything because he couldn't. His chest was tight and full of something that was neither joy nor sadness, and yet at the same time both of those things, and more... much, much more. Oh yes, he thought, I will remember you....

Ann was sorry to find herself at her own front gate. She didn't want to go back into her house and face Sunny's moods. Not tonight. Tonight she just wanted to feel the warmth of Niall's hand, the big, solid strength of his body... for a little while longer... she dared not think of forever. When he let go of her hand to unlatch the gate she wanted to protest like a disappointed child, to cry out loud, No! Not yet, not yet!

Instead she said lightly, ''Well, shall we have that ice cream now? And some tea. I bought you some tea, you know. I'm sorry, I couldn't find... what was that kind you asked for?''

Niall chuckled. ''Darjeeling. But never mind. Whatever you have will be fine.... How is your head?''

"My head?" She turned to look at him. He was standing two steps below her so that his eyes were almost on a level with hers. It gave her a giddy feeling, like climbing one rung too high on a ladder.

He smiled; the ladder swayed. "The wine...you were light-headed. Are you feeling better now?"

"Oh...yes," she lied, "the walk helped a lot. Thank you...." She felt as if she'd drunk the whole bottle of wine; she was shaking inside, hot and cold at the same time, clinging desperately to dignity and sanity while the winds of her emotions buffeted her like a new-leafed willow. She told herself, Annie, don't be a fool! He's a stranger. He doesn't belong here. In a few days he'll be gone, and in another week he won't remember your name!

She knew it was true—she knew it. But something in her cried, like that stubborn, disappointed child, I don't care, I don't care! And it took every bit of willpower she had to turn from him and push open the door.

Just inside the door she stopped and stood very still. Anger washed through her, bringing with it a different kind of cold, a different kind of light-headedness. From a distance she heard her own voice say calmly, "Well. I see Sunny hasn't gotten around to clearing the table yet."

On shaking legs she crossed the room, unbuttoning her coat on the way, and knocked on her daughter's bedroom door. "Sunny, will you come out here for a minute please? I'd like to talk to you." She waited, counting slowly to ten, painfully conscious of Niall's big, silent presence there, somewhere in the room behind her.

Sunny opened the door, looking tousled and put-upon. "Yeah, what is it?"

"Why didn't you do what I asked you to do?"

Sunny's expression changed to one of bland innocence. "Oh, did you tell me to do something? I guess I didn't hear you."

Ann's palms tingled. She clasped them tightly together. She managed to keep her voice low and steady as she said,

"You know very well what I told you to do. I told you to clear the table. I want you to come and do it now."

The innocence vanished. Sunny folded her arms on her chest and adopted a stance of classic adolescent intractability. "Look, he's *your* date, not mine," she said rudely, gesturing with her head in Niall's direction. "If you want to make a fool of yourself, that's your business. Just leave me out of it, okay?"

"Sunny—" The slam of the door cut off the rest of it. Without another word, Ann turned and walked to the table, where she began stacking dishes with blind disregard for their preservation. She felt fragile herself, and very near to breaking.

"I'll take those," Niall said quietly. His hand covered hers, just in time to rescue a toppling wineglass.

Ann stood for a moment with her head bowed, unable to look at him, not wanting to imagine what he must be thinking. Then she straightened her shoulders. What did it matter, after all? she thought dismally. Sunny was right— she had been making a fool of herself.

Picking up the platter with the congealed remains of the roast, she said, "Thank you, that's very kind of you," in a clear, calm voice, and headed for the kitchen.

With narrowed eyes, Rankin watched her go, then picked up a precarious pile of plates and followed. He found her bustling with industry and concentration between sink and stove and refrigerator, taking great care not to look directly at him. He deposited the plates in the already crowded sink and intercepted her.

"Hey, take it easy," he murmured, gently removing a carving knife from her fingers. "The dishes aren't going anywhere."

She gave a short, humiliated laugh and for the second time that night said, "I'm sorry."

"Sorry for what?"

Her voice was muffled. "That must have been embarrassing for you."

"I don't get embarrassed," Rankin said easily. "I am curious, though."

"Curious? About what?"

"Why do you let her get away with it?"

She turned away from him and said stiffly, "It's very complicated. Adolescents are—"

"What's complicated about it? You told her to do something, she didn't do it, and you let her get away with it."

"Look," Ann flared at him, sparks of anger in her eyes and a tremor in her voice, "I don't expect you to understand. You don't know anything about teenagers, you said so yourself. I don't think you have any business—"

"I know about discipline," Rankin said quietly. "And I know when someone's crying out for a little of it."

"How do *you* know what my child needs? Yesterday you didn't even know her! What gives you the right—"

"I believe I have the right." Rankin cut through her anger with slow, deliberate words. "Because if it hadn't been for me, she wouldn't be here with you today. Had you forgotten that? And as for knowing what your child needs, I know because she told me."

"She... told you?"

"In her own way." He paused, then said it coldly, flatly, knowing how it would hurt her. "She told me you don't care what she does. It looks to me as if she may be right."

Ann's face went pale as parchment, so that her freckles stood out like spatters of brown ink. "How dare you?" she whispered. "How *dare* you stand there and tell me I don't care about my child?" Her voice broke on the last word. Tears slipped down her cheeks and she swiped angrily at them with her fingers. "I love her more than anything in this world, do you understand me? I don't know what I'd do if anything—"

She turned from him abruptly, shoulders rigid, head bowed. Her hair parted on the back of her neck and slithered forward like honey-colored curtains to hide her face, leaving her nape exposed. Above the thick, fuzzy material of her dress it looked naked, and unbelievably vulnerable.

Pain caught Rankin unaware, like a sneaky punch to the solar plexus. It was an unfamiliar pain. He didn't know what to call it or what was causing it, but it moved him to reach out, against his own best judgment, and put his hand on that slender, fragile stem. It felt warm, and velvety soft. His fingers moved on the sides of her neck, gently stroking. He felt the ripple of her swallow. And the pain inside him grew.

He whispered, "Ann...please."

Responding to the slightest pressure of his fingers, she turned, hesitantly at first, almost fearfully, searching his face, asking questions with her glistening, tear-filled eyes.

Rankin had meant to apologize, but now, looking into those eyes, he found that he could not; there was too much honesty in them. He knew that every word he'd said had been calculated and deliberate, and that he'd achieved exactly what he'd set out to achieve, so how could he be sorry? He was adept at cracking people, skilled at extracting the truth beneath their facades, and Ann had been easier than most. He hadn't anticipated the tears, but he found he wasn't really sorry for those, either, even though he knew that they were responsible in some way for his own pain. He studied them intently, almost clinically, touched their moisture with the tips of his fingers.

"Don't cry," he admonished her gently, and cradling her upturned face between his hands, lightly kissed her.

Her lips were petal-soft, full and lush, trembling and warm...a woman's lips...a woman's mouth. It had been a long time.... He lifted his head just slightly, tasting the salt-sweet moisture of her tears, heard the little catch in her breathing, felt the sharp intake of breath, and then the suspense, the waiting. Her parted lips trembled there, just the width of a wish away from his own. He waited for her to pull away, willed himself to do the same. But instead he felt her fingers touch his face, lightly, cool as a breeze, with so much tenderness and giving in them....

It was too much. Even tempered steel has its breaking point. Hadn't he just said that? And kissing Ann was out of the question—he'd said that, too—but suddenly he knew he was going to kiss her anyway. With an inarticulate murmur of apology—to himself, to her—he lowered his mouth over hers and felt her open and respond to him like a flower to sunlight. As he'd known she would.

The pain exploded inside him and then dissipated, leaving only heat, the writhing, white-hot kind that can scour a man's mind clean and in an instant make him forget all right and reason. Both shocked and exhilarated to discover that he was still capable of such passion—a folly he'd assumed to be the sole province of youth—he gave in to it for a time. Briefly, he allowed himself to sink into her mouth, to plunge his tongue into its hot, sweet depths, savor the feel of her body against his, and to think of the natural progression of what he was doing now—his body and hers, himself inside her, the heart-pounding release that would leave him spent . . . drained. A primitive fantasy, simple and uncomplicated. Male and female . . . as natural and right as breathing.

Only this was *Ann*. It was neither right nor simple. It was out of the question.

She made a small, helpless sound—a whimper—and that helped a little, reminding him of her vulnerability, reminding him that she played the game by a different set of rules. He withdrew from her slowly, trying to lessen the shock for them both, swirling his tongue sensuously through her mouth and over her lips, leaving them glazed and swollen . . . and incredibly inviting. He groaned softly and closed his eyes, but the image of her mouth, the feel of it, the taste of it, was already burned on all his senses. He skimmed his hands down her sides, feeling her warmth and willingness through the down-soft fabric of her dress. He curled his fingers into the material, fighting the urge to haul it up, or down, anywhere at all so long as it was out of the way and not standing between him and her satin-sweet skin. . . .

Gripping her shoulders hard, he lifted his head and put her firmly away from him. Her hands came up as if in protest, briefly hovered over the front of his sweater, then settled on the lapels of his jacket.

He said, "Ann, I take full responsibility for this." She shook her head. He went on, speaking harshly, rapidly, not giving her a chance to say anything at all, knowing that if she put into words what was in her face, he would never be able to resist her. "No, it was inexcusable." He took a deep breath and forced the words past his lips. "I think I'd better go. I have outstayed my welcome. Thank you for a lovely evening."

At that she snatched her hands away from his jacket and touched the fingers of one of them to her mouth, trying as unobtrusively as possible to wipe his essence from her lips. With that more or less accomplished, she lifted her head, shook back her hair and said carefully, "You're welcome."

Rankin watched her struggle for pride and composure and ached for her with every syllable.

"I'm so glad you could come," she went on, her voice light and even. "I'm only sorry you can't stay for tea."

It was so ludicrous, he almost burst out laughing. He caught himself in time, but then, when he looked at Ann he was certain he saw the same glimmer in her eyes, the same tug at the corners of her mouth, quickly controlled. It surprised him, and made it better, somehow. Not all right, but ... better.

He said good night to her there in her kitchen and let himself out. At the bottom of the steps he paused and bent down to rub the old dog's ears and receive a tongue swipe across the back of his hand in return. Then he straightened and walked on down the walk, with a sprig of lilac in his jacket pocket and a lightness in his heart that hadn't been there in a long, long time.

"Well, this is as far as I go," Bill Clemson said as he turned off the motor. He leaned back in the driver's seat of

Rankin's rented Ford and released a pent-up breath. "Sure do wish I was coming with you."

"Sorry, my friend. I am accustomed to working alone." Rankin opened the car door and reached into the back seat for his gear.

Bill ran a hand over his hair and shook his head. "Yeah, but you told me you were out of shape."

Rankin's only reply to that was a dry and dangerous chuckle as he opened a small flat metal container and began to smear his face and neck with lamp black. Bill turned to watch him, one arm on the back of the seat, one draped across the steering wheel. After a moment he remarked, "Doesn't look to me like you've forgotten too much."

"Some things you don't forget," Rankin muttered. "Like riding a bicycle."

"Yeah—and sex."

Rankin glanced at him, but the sheriff's grin was without hidden meanings, so he just laughed softly and went on methodically checking his equipment and supplies. He'd always been careful; he liked to leave as little as possible to chance.

Bill shifted restlessly. "You know if you get caught you're on your own. I don't know you, I was never here."

Rankin laughed dryly. "I've heard *that* before," he said as he adjusted a pair of goggles, then pulled a black knit cap over his hair. The goggles were state-of-the-art U.S. military commando issue; they would help his night vision considerably. He put on his gloves and was about to shrug into the pack when Bill put out a hand and stopped him.

"Listen, Rankin..." He squirmed and coughed and finally came out with, "I want you to know how much I appreciate what you're doing." He stopped there, but after a brief, narrow-eyed appraisal Rankin decided there was something more the sheriff had to say. So he acknowledged the thank you with a shrug and fiddled with the fastenings on his pack while he waited for the rest.

"Rankin, maybe this isn't the time or the place to say this, but I'm gonna say it anyway." But the sheriff was still having trouble with it, apparently; it took some more throat clearing before he could proceed, and when he did, Rankin knew it wasn't a law officer talking, but a private man who respected other people's privacy when he could. "The other day I told you I could spot a man on the run, and you never denied it. Look, I don't know what you're running from. Hell, maybe I don't want to know." He grinned, the lawman again, for an instant. "Long as your record's clean. But . . . I do know this. Everybody's got to stop running sometime. And if you're looking for a place to light, this isn't a bad place to do it."

Unexpectedly moved, Rankin opened his mouth to reply. The sheriff held up his hand, stopping him. "Just think about it . . . while you're out there. If you need a job, I can always use a good man. And if you don't—" He shrugged. "Well, the air's clean, the people are friendly, and the fishing's the best in the world. Hell, I sound like the damn chamber of commerce. Rankin—" He stuck out his hand; Rankin took it and gripped it hard. "Good luck. I'll see you back here tomorrow . . . nineteen hundred hours. If you're not here, I'll be back the next day, same place, same time. If you're still not here . . . well, I guess I'll have my reason, then, won't I?"

Rankin chuckled and murmured, *"Auf Wiedersehen."* He slammed the door and stood back with a wave, then watched the car's taillights disappear around a bend in the road, leaving him alone on the mountain.

He stood very still for a moment, listening to the sound of the wind in the pines. Then he shifted his backpack, adjusted his goggles and set off toward the north, into the trees.

Six

Sunny was late. She wasn't there when Ann got home from work, which wasn't unusual in itself. But her books weren't there, either, and there wasn't any snack mess in the kitchen. And Sarge hadn't been fed and watered.

Ann told herself there wasn't any reason to worry. She looked for a note, wracked her brain trying to remember if there was some school function she'd forgotten about, then told herself Sunny must have stopped off at a friend's house on the way home from school. She'd be home soon. There was no reason to worry.

She thought of calling Sunny's friends. She hated calling them, hated the cold, sweaty palms and the butterflies in her stomach and the inevitable answer: "No, I haven't seen her, Mrs. Severn, I'm sorry..." She hated hearing that cool lilt of pity in the voices of people she'd known all her life, hated imagining their thoughts: Poor Ann...first Mark and now Sunny. What a shame the child is turning out just like her father....

Fear rolled through her like a cold winter storm. She wouldn't call just yet. It was early, not even dark. Sunny had probably gone to the local pizza parlor with friends, and just lost track of time. She'd wait a while longer. Right now, Sarge needed to be fed. Yes—she'd do that first, and *then* she'd start making those calls....

When she put his food dish down in its usual place beside the faucet, Sarge looked at her with his soft brown eyes and thumped his tail twice, but didn't get up.

"What's the matter, old Sarge?" Ann said softly. "Not hungry tonight?" The dog lifted his muzzle into her hand and licked it. She sighed and dropped to her knees in the dirt beside him, wrapping her arms around his neck and burying her face in his shaggy black coat, as she'd done so often during the nightmare days just before and after Mark's death.

"Oh, Sarge," she whispered, and then was silent. That was the thing about dogs—you didn't have to try to explain the pain inside you...the terrible loneliness, the helplessness, the fear. They just seemed to know when you needed comforting; they never needed to know the reasons why.

Sometimes she wondered what she was going to do when Sarge wasn't around anymore. He was old, and dogs didn't live forever. She wondered about Sunny, too. Sunny couldn't remember a time when Sarge hadn't been there, serving faithfully as her pillow, playmate and protector. Mark had brought the puppy home not long after Sunny was born; how well Ann remembered that day, and that roly poly little black teddy bear with a white spot under his chin and tan thumbprints over his eyes, too young even to eat by himself.

"But that's the idea," Mark had said when Ann protested. "He's a special kind of shepherd, honey. He'll grow up with the baby and he'll think she's his own family." And he'd told her about the sheepherders in England, and how they would take the puppies from their mothers before they were weaned and raise them with the lambs, on sheep milk, so they would adopt the herd as their own. Ann could still remember Mark saying, "You'll never have to worry about Sunny as long as this dog is around. He'll guard her with his life, and she'll never be alone."

Alone. Sometimes she thought that was the thing Mark had feared most—being alone. In high school he'd been so outgoing, always surrounded by a group of friends, teammates. But after Vietnam he'd seemed isolated, somehow, as if he'd felt that what had happened to him over there set him apart from other people, that there were things inside him he couldn't share with anyone, not even his closest friends. Not even her. Little by little he'd shut himself off from her, walled himself up inside his own private hell, and she hadn't been able to reach him no matter how hard she tried. And God knew, she'd tried. She'd tried so hard. Maybe if she hadn't tried so hard, if she'd been more patient, if she'd just given him more time, more space . . .

It wasn't your fault. There was nothing you could have done.

People had told her that after . . . after *it* happened— counselors, ministers, friends. Mark just wasn't strong enough, they'd told her. He didn't have the inner strength to deal with the things that happened to him over there. Some people are like that. Some are strong inside, some aren't. But *you*, Ann, you are strong. You're a survivor.

Oh, yes, *she* was strong, and a survivor. But what about Sunny? Sunny was Mark's child, too.

"Oh, Sarge . . . I don't know what to do."

But tonight, for some reason, there was no comfort to be found in the old dog's passive sympathy. Ann stood up, brushing the knees of her slacks, and went into the house to begin telephoning Sunny's friends.

Headlights slashed briefly through the trees and were extinguished; the car rolled on a few yards into the clearing before its engine died with a small, asthmatic wheeze, leaving both the darkness and the wind's whisper to resume as if they'd never been interrupted.

A full minute ticked by, measured in pulse beats, before the door opened, splashing light across the uneven ground. A man got out and stood in the light, one arm resting on the roof of the car while he scanned the darkness.

Rankin straightened unhurriedly, pushed away from the trunk of the yellow pine that concealed him, and crossed the clearing . . . cat-silent, cat-quick.

"You're late, my friend."

Bill Clemson jumped and swore. "Geez, don't *do* that, man! If I was armed I would've probably shot you."

Rankin laughed softly. "Ah, but I know you're not armed."

Bill snapped his fingers. "That's right. Forgot about those damn glasses. How'd they work, by the way?"

"Fine," Rankin grunted. "They worked great." He peeled them off and tossed them into the backseat, then shrugged off the backpack and dropped it into the trunk. "Let's get out of here."

Bill gave him a look as he slid in behind the wheel and said casually, "Everything go okay?"

"Tell you about it on the way." Rankin slammed the trunk and went around to the passenger side, grinning at Bill as he sank into the seat. "Right now, what I want most is a shower."

The sheriff grinned back at him. "Yeah, you look like hell—nothing but teeth and eyes." They laughed together like co-conspirators, like schoolboys who'd just pulled off a grand and glorious mischief.

Rankin felt like a schoolboy—exuberant and tireless, full of energy. *Young.* Lately, sitting behind a desk, nursing an ulcer, watching his hair turn gray and trying his best to keep in shape on exercise bikes and weight machines, he'd missed this—the exhilaration, the danger. The special sense of purpose that came from doing something he believed in.

"You were right about one thing," he said, and reached automatically for a cigarette, as had been his habit when he was coming in off a job, still keyed up and on an adrenaline high. He caught himself and leaned his head back against the seat, swearing and muttering under his breath.

Bill looked at him. "How long since you quit?"

Rankin gave a snort of self-disgust. "Six weeks. Damn— I thought I had it licked, but these last few days . . . I don't know."

"I got news for you," Bill said with a sympathetic chuckle, "it doesn't get much better. I quit cold turkey three years ago, and I *still* get the urge. Some things you just never get out of your system, I guess. So get your mind off it. What am I right about?"

"Well, those people are definitely getting ready for the end."

"Yeah," Bill said grimly. "The only thing I want to know is, *whose* end—theirs or the Almighty's? You get anything concrete?"

Rankin jerked a thumb toward the rear of the car. "We'll see soon enough. It's all there in my backpack. Do you have any topographical maps of the area?"

"In my office." Bill glanced at him sideways. "I'd hate to get caught with you in the station looking like that."

Rankin's reply was soft, but vibrant with an old, remembered thrill. "Then I guess we'll just have to make sure we don't get caught, won't we?"

"I guess that's something else you never really lose," Bill commented as they drove down the mountain. He glanced over at Rankin. "You know what I mean, don't you? You can get hooked on this kind of thing—the adrenaline high. It's like a drug—worse than cigarettes. Tough to give it up."

"Yeah," Rankin said on a long exhalation, looking out the window. That was what he was afraid of. He doubted there'd be much personal stake in industrial espionage.

Ann drove slowly through the streets, her hands cramped around the steering wheel, shoulders hunched and stiff with tension. Her breathing was audible and panic-stricken; her eyes were hot and dry from the strain of trying to penetrate the darkness, and from sorting through crowds in the brightly lit places where the young people gathered. Crying might have helped, but her fear was too overwhelming for tears.

Now and then the fear was displaced by anger. She'd think, How could she *do* this to me? How could she put me through this? Some day, please God, let her have children of her own, so she will know how this feels!

And then the fear would return, and she would pray, through dry-eyed whimpers, please God, just let her be all right.

She'd driven by the high school first, but the gymnasium was dark and deserted. For a while she tried to talk herself into believing that Sunny might have gone to an out-of-town game with friends—even though to have done so without letting her mother know was thoughtlessness bordering on cruelty. At one time, not so long ago, it would have been a logical assumption. But not lately. Not since Sunny had become so moody, so withdrawn, so alienated from all her friends, and most especially from Will Clemson, who was captain of the basketball team and its high point scorer. No. Ann felt quite certain that the basketball game was the last place Sunny would have gone.

Finally, almost inevitably, she found herself on the highway, heading south, out of town. And now, with the highway stretching arrow-straight before her and nothing but dark sky and stars overhead, with the mountains a great brooding blackness beyond the car windows, the loneliness overwhelmed her and the tears began to slip silently down her cheeks.

She was certain that Sunny had run away again. And this time she hadn't taken Sarge along to slow her down. This time there wouldn't be a mysterious and enigmatic stranger named Rankin to rescue her and bring her safely home.

Rankin. She thought of him now as she had almost constantly for the last two days, with a quivering in her stomach and a mind full of questions. Who was he? *Where* was he? She knew he must still be in town, because she'd overheard Allie Henshaw, who worked at the Whispering

Pines Motel, telling someone at the bank this morning that his car was still there, and that he hadn't checked out or given any indication that he was planning to do so. But Allie hadn't seen him for several days. No one had. Everyone had looked at Ann as if they expected her to have information they didn't, and she'd had to face them all down and pretend indifference.

"I really don't know what Mr. Rankin's business is," she'd said coolly in response to their questions. "It's certainly none of mine."

No, Niall Rankin's business wasn't any of hers. He was a stranger just passing through, like the hundreds of other strangers who drove through Pinetree every day on their way to somewhere else. He was only a sojourner in her world and in her life. Like the panther in the barnyard, she thought, and felt a sharp and wrenching sense of loss. She knew she was probably never going to see him again, but like that elusive night visitor, he'd left his footprints behind. Only difference was, footprints in snow were soon gone, but she didn't think she was ever going to forget the imprint of this particular stranger's mouth...and hands....

The lurch in her stomach evoked by those memories put a stop to her tears and jolted her back to reality. *Sunny.* All that mattered was Sunny. She had to stay calm and stop running around like a crazy person, accomplishing nothing. If Sunny had run away again she had several hours head start, and if she hadn't she might even be home by now. And if she wasn't at home waiting for her... Well, as much as Ann hated to, as much as she might fight the idea, she knew it was time to go to the police.

She decided to go straight to Bill's office. It was faster than going home first and calling from there, and then having to wait for someone to come. And this way she wouldn't have to explain the sheriff's car in front of her house on a Friday night, which was no small consideration in a town the size of Pinetree. Not that it wouldn't be all over town by noon tomorrow anyway.

She parked in the dirt lot behind the sheriff's station and went in through the officer's entrance. She'd been here so many times with Mark, or with Bill's wife Patty, and even by herself a time or two, unofficially, as a friend. But this was different.

Outwardly calm, but with a wildly pounding heart, she walked down the narrow hallway, past the locker room and the lavatory. One of the young deputies, whose name she couldn't recall, was in the alcove that held the microwave, coffeemaker and pop machine, pouring himself a cup of coffee. He seemed a little startled to see her, but before he could say anything, she said, "Is Bill in his office?"

The young deputy waved his cup and grunted an affirmative.

Ann thanked him, pushed open the door, took two steps and stopped cold.

Bill Clemson wasn't alone. There was a stranger in his office. And not just any stranger.

It was, Ann thought wonderingly, a scene straight out of a movie—something about jewel thieves or spies, one of those cat-and-mouse, counterespionage thrillers Mark had loved so much when they were kids. There was Bill, out of uniform in plaid shirt and jeans, looking as if he'd just come back from a hunting trip. And there was the stranger, dressed all in black from the toes of his hiking boots to his turtleneck sweater. He had something black rubbed on his skin, too, every visible inch of it except for a narrow stripe across his forehead where a black knit ski cap had rubbed it clean. The cap itself was sitting there on the desk, just to the right of the large, spread-out map the men were poring over. When Ann walked in they both jumped and looked up, like boys caught with their hands in the cookie jar. She might have laughed if it hadn't been so obvious that it wasn't a joke, that neither Bill nor the man with him were pleased to see her.

It all happened so quickly. Uncertain whether to stay or go, Ann faltered and mumbled, "Oh, I'm sorry."

Bill said, "Ah, geez, Annie," and swiped a hand over his hair.

The stranger just said quietly, "Come in, please, and close the door." The sound of his voice, with its unmistakable accent, gave Ann her second shock of the evening.

The stranger was Niall Rankin.

She hadn't recognized him at first, because he was a very different Niall Rankin from the one that had haunted her thoughts for days, waking and sleeping...the one whose mouth she still tasted, whose rough hands she still felt on her body and longed to feel again...whose touch was so compelling she'd known she'd walk through fire if he'd asked it, and so tender it made her heart ache. The one whose smiling eyes had charmed her across a wineglass, and whose body she'd felt as he walked beside her in the dark, a solid, comforting warmth.

This Niall Rankin wasn't smiling; his eyes were cold and hard as bits of blue glass. Altogether, he looked lean, fit and dangerous as a Doberman.

"I'm sorry," Ann said again, swallowing nervously, her back flat against the door. "I didn't know anybody was here."

"Hell, the damage is done, you might as well come in," Bill said with a lack of graciousness forgivable between lifelong friends. "What are you doing here anyway? Something wrong? Ah—" He swore briefly and succinctly and shook his head. "It's Sunny again, isn't it?"

Ann nodded and glanced at Niall. It was a mistake. Meeting those cold blue eyes was like running headlong into a wall of ice. Her breath left her and her knees turned to water. Wrenching her eyes away from his was like pulling away from freezing metal; she felt as if she'd left a piece of herself behind. Torn and burning, she turned back to Bill, stammering like a child.

"She didn't come home after school. She hasn't called, she didn't leave a note.... I don't know where she is, Bill, I've looked everywhere. I think—I'm afraid she's run away again. I don't know what else to think—"

The two men looked at each other. Bill came around his desk and took her by the arms, saying in a more kindly tone, "Hey, take it easy. It's going to be all right. First thing you've got to do is stay calm, okay? Are you sure she didn't just go to the game?"

Ann shook him off. She was already upset, and seeing Niall again, inexplicably dressed up like a cat burglar and in a place where she'd never in a million years have expected to see him, had upset her even more. She was in no mood to be patronized. "I am calm," she said, speaking in a low, even voice to prove she was. "Sunny is gone. I don't think she went to the game, I think she's run away again. I would like you to help me find her. Please."

Bill glanced over at Niall, who was standing behind the desk, arms folded, silent as a shadow. Then he puffed up his cheeks and let the air out slowly. "Okay...here's what we're gonna do. I'll take down the information—what she was wearing, when you saw her last." He paused, rummaging under the map for a notebook and pencil. "And then I want you to go home and see if she's there before I go ahead and put this out. Will you do that for me, Annie?"

Ann reined in her temper, took a deep breath and told him all she could remember about what Sunny had worn to school that morning. Bill wrote it all down, then tucked the notebook into his pocket and took her by the arm.

"Okay, this should do it. Let me get somebody to run you home. You call me when you get there and let me know if she's still not back."

"I have my car," Ann said.

"Leave it here. You're upset. Let me—"

"I'm not upset."

"You are too." He gave her cheek a big-brotherly swipe with his knuckles. "Look at you—you look like hell. Let me get Art to take you, he's not doing anything." He opened the door and yelled into the hallway, "Hey, Art—"

"I'll take her home," Niall said, speaking for the first time since inviting her into the office. When Bill started to protest he added quietly, "I think we're finished here anyway... for the time being."

There was a subtle emphasis on the last part that wasn't lost on Ann, even as distracted as she was. She found it vaguely irritating, like being on the outside of an inside joke. She found it even more irritating when Niall paused in the doorway as they were leaving to say something to Bill under his breath. She caught the words "camera," and "Monday."

She *hated* being left out of things. Though she'd been raised the only offspring of cattle ranchers and rodeo cowboys and had been taught at an early age to ride and fish and handle a gun as well as any boy, those people were also barely a generation removed from the horse and buggy, and a world where values were old-fashioned, and the barriers between men's and women's worlds clearly defined and well-nigh unbridgeable. So she'd learned even earlier that there were certain times and places and activities that belonged only to "menfolks." That men had a language that was only between themselves, and certain business she could never be privy to. She knew that and accepted it, but she didn't have to like it.

So Niall Rankin had business with Bill Clemson—secret business. Men's business. So what? It was none of her business.

But she was curious. And deep in her heart she resented it.

"Do you want to drive, or shall I?" Rankin asked as he held the back door for her.

She shot him a look as she slid past him and said coolly, "I can drive. Thank you anyway."

That was fine with Rankin. He watched her crunch ahead of him across the dirt parking lot, liking the way she looked in slacks and enjoying the familiar pull and tug of response in his belly and loins. Her manner, as she pointed out her Bronco and waited for him to climb in on the passenger side, was as cool and impersonal as her voice. Which was probably just as well. He had always come in off a mission keyed up and hungry, and it had been a long time since he'd wanted any woman as much as he wanted *this* woman, right here, and right now....

The night was dark and cold and smelled of dust and hard driven motor vehicles and charbroiled meat from a fast-food place down the street. There was no reason why he should be thinking about a recent night, one that smelled of lilacs and a sweet, clean woman instead. Or of the two nights he'd just spent in pine-scented loneliness, remembering the taste of her, the feel of her body in his hands, of her hands on his face.... He looked at those same hands now, small hands curled on the steering wheel of her Bronco, and shuddering inside, cursed himself for having a conscience.

It was a damn good thing she was giving him the cold shoulder, he thought grimly, small wonder considering what had happened the last time they'd been together. A good thing, and small wonder... and yet there was a part of him that was sorry.

He made himself stop looking at her then, and cursed himself for not having the good sense to stay away from her, for underestimating his attraction to her, for putting himself through this adolescent torment.

Ann didn't say a word on the short drive home. She drove with great concentration, nursing the tiny ember of her resentment into a good, steady blaze of anger she could use as protection against the more frightening emotions that lurked in the shadows—her fear for Sunny, and whatever it was that made her heart pound and her knees grow weak whenever Niall Rankin was around.

She parked the Bronco in the driveway, got out and slammed her door without waiting for Niall. He was there, though, standing on the bottom step as she reached the top one, his head level with her shoulder.

"You don't lock your door?" he remarked as she pushed it open.

Ann just looked at him and walked into the kitchen. It was exactly as she had left it—the light on over the stove, no crumbs on the counter, no milk glass in the sink. Obviously, Sunny hadn't come home yet. Not giving herself time to think about that, Ann dropped her keys on the table and made straight for the sink. She collected a towel and a bottle of dish detergent, turned and thrust them at Niall.

"I expect you'd like to wash," she said tersely.

He looked at the towel, clean, fluffy-white, printed with farm animals in unlikely pastels, then at his blackened hands. His teeth flashed white for an instant before he said mildly, "Are you sure you want me to do that here?"

She let her eyes flick across his face, then drop. Her stomach gave a queer little hiccup, and she pulled her eyes back up again. Elegant and immaculate in cream-colored cashmere and doeskin suede, Niall Rankin had been an assault on her senses—on any woman's senses. But she could handle that. After all, she wasn't a dewy-eyed teenager, to be bowled over by a set of broad shoulders and a winning smile. Niall Rankin in fighting black, red-eyed and dirty and sporting a three-day beard, was something else entirely—something rough, and earthy, and dangerous. *Exciting*. His appeal wasn't to the senses but to something even more fundamental, something primitive and wild deep within her that she hadn't known about until this moment, and which she wasn't at all sure she could control.

"You're right," she said, turning on her heel. "You'd better use the shower."

She showed him where it was, told him the towels were in the left-hand cupboard and then got out of his way. Or tried to. He stopped her in the bathroom doorway, one coal-black hand lightly touching her arm, and said softly, "Are you going to call Bill?"

His chest was about a foot from the end of her nose, so broad it filled her whole field of vision and made her head swim. She nodded, swallowed a chunk of dessert and murmured, "In a minute. I want to look in her room again, just to make sure she didn't leave me a note. I was upset...maybe I missed it."

Something—his knuckles, a finger, perhaps—brushed her cheek, momentarily stopping her breathing; she marveled that hands so big and rough could possess so gentle a touch. The bathroom door clicked shut and a moment later she heard the shower. Ann retreated on wobbly legs, giving herself no chance to dwell on the images conjured up by that sound....

In Sunny's room she turned on the light and was instantly swamped by a wave of indefinable grief and sadness. "Oh, baby," she whispered. "Sunny...where are you? What's happening to you?"

From the grungy, threadbare panda on the bed to the soccer trophies on the dresser, to the nursery lamp shaped like a clown holding balloons that Sunny still used as a night-light and the poster on the wall that said, "Trespassers Will Be Eaten..." the room was a warehouse of memories. Sunny never threw anything away. There on her bookshelves were all the books Ann had ever bought her, a chronicle of a little girl's growing up. It was all there: Little Golden Books, Dr. Seuss and Sesame Street, Garfield and Peanuts, the hardcover animal story classics Ann used to read aloud to her—*Lassie, Come Home, My Friend Flicka,* and *Bambi.* All the Black Stallion books, of course, and a few Nancy Drew mysteries. There was Beverly Cleary and Judy Blume, who had given way, in junior high school, to the teen romances that now took up most of the top shelf.

Ann smiled as she ran one finger over the well-worn spines of those books, remembering how quickly it had happened—from seventh to eighth grade, just like that. Suddenly the little tomboy who'd cared more for dogs than boys was developing crushes and worrying about her weight. And then, about the time Sunny started high school...

Ann held herself still, listening, her insides jumping like crickets on hot sand. She'd heard something.

There it was again. Sarge was barking.

She made it to the living room window and peeked out through the curtains just in time to see a car drive away. A car she didn't recognize. Ice cold and shaking with a bewildering mixture of relief and rage, she watched Sunny wave to the disappearing taillights, stoop to give Sarge a hug, and then rush on up the walk with a bouncy, half-skipping step Ann hadn't seen in a long, long time.

Sunny came through the door, cheeks flushed, eyes shining, hair swinging, and chirped, "Oh—hi, Mom. Still up?"

Ann felt like a post. She heard a distant voice say woodenly, "It's after midnight. Where have you been?"

Sunny's eyes were wide and innocent. "With some friends. I went to their place after school. I didn't think you'd mind."

"You didn't think I'd mind . . ."

She shrugged. "Yeah—you always work late on Friday anyway." Her face had a closed look, at once bland and evasive. Ann had a sudden, shameful urge to slap her.

"I work until six," she said carefully, struggling to keep her emotions out of her voice. "Why didn't you call me and let me know where you were?"

"They don't have a phone. Mom, it is so *neat*." She dropped her backpack onto the couch and threw out her arms in a gesture of unbridled enthusiasm, which was more animation than Ann had seen her display in months. In fact, she couldn't remember the last time she'd heard her daughter use the word *neat*. "You wouldn't believe it—these people are *so nice*. They live up in the mountains, you know, at that religious camp? They don't have telephones or TV or any of that stuff—they don't believe in it. They're trying to live like people used to, a long time ago—except they have electricity—but they make their own, from this waterfall, so it doesn't hurt the environment, or anything...."

Her voice trailed off, and the childish sparkle in her eyes changed, became something else entirely. Something that matched the brittle edge of sarcasm in her voice as she said sweetly, "Well, this is certainly cozy."

"Hello, Sunny," Niall said pleasantly.

Seven

He had come in while they were talking, in that silent way he had...moving without a ripple, just suddenly *there*. He was dressed but barefooted and drying his hair with a towel, making it very clear where he'd been and what he'd been doing.

As Sunny's lips curved in a cynical smile, Ann's anger with her cooled in a wash of parental guilt. It did no good to tell herself that Niall's presence in her bathroom was completely innocent: *she* knew her own thoughts had been anything but.

She'd always thought there was something...well, *sweet* about a man fresh from the shower. That there was something about wet hair and the smell of soap that gave a man a kind of boyish innocence, that made even the roughest, toughest man seem less threatening, more manageable. Not this man. Maybe it was the black clothes, or the beard-shadowed jaws, or the cold blue glitter of his eyes, but whatever the reason, Niall Rankin looked about as sweet and manageable as a wet leopard.

"Uh..." was all Ann could think of to say. A pulse throbbed heavily in the pit of her stomach. Her thoughts and emotions were hopelessly tangled, her responsibilities as a parent grappling desperately with her needs as a woman, needs that had been on the shelf so long she'd all but forgotten them. And what a time for those needs to re-surface, she thought with chagrin. In the middle of a crisis with Sunny. It couldn't be worse. It was beyond inconvenient; it was impossible. She couldn't think of Niall Rankin right now, and his mysterious business with Bill, and the way it made her feel just to look at him. She had her hands full with her own business. Her child. Sunny—that was all that mattered.

Oh, but for just a moment the woman in her cried, What about me? I matter, too!

"Niall was just leaving," she said, her voice steady and calm. "I was looking for you and...he brought me home."

"Oh, really?" Sunny widened her eyes guilelessly. "He's good at that, isn't he?"

Ann had her mouth open ready to defend, to explain, when she glanced at Niall and caught the almost imperceptible shake of his head. She clamped her jaws so hard they hurt.

Sunny favored them each with a sweet little kitty-cat smile. "Well, I guess I'll go to bed now...leave you two alone. I'm sure you'd like that. G'night, Mom. 'Night...*Niall.*"

Ann waited until she heard Sunny's bedroom door click shut, then slowly uncurled her clenched fists. Her fingers felt cramped and her palms were clammy.

"You shouldn't have tried to explain," Niall said mildly. "You don't owe her an explanation." The towel he'd been using to dry his hair—*her* towel—was looped around his neck, with his hands still holding the ends of it. His stance was relaxed, confident.

Ann, on the other hand, was shaking like a leaf; she wasn't sure why—delayed reaction, perhaps, or anger. She only knew that her emotions were raw, her temper on hair trigger, that she felt like a dog with a sore tooth.

"Are you telling me how to discipline my daughter?" she said through a dangerous stillness.

One of Niall's eyebrows shot up, almost colliding with the dark, wet spikes of hair that had fallen across his forehead. He gave a short, sardonic laugh. "Were you going to?"

Anger was such a cleansing emotion, Ann thought. Simple and uncomplicated. She inhaled through her nose, balled her hands into fists and snapped, "You have no right to judge me."

"We had this conversation the other night in your kitchen," Niall said with maddening self-control, using one end of the towel to mop an errant drip from his forehead. He shook his head, then gave her a brief, humorless smile. "And in spite of what I said then, you're probably right— I don't have any right. In any case, I'm not judging you. How could I? I've never been in your shoes." His voice softened without losing any of its intensity. "But I think I know when someone is getting in over her head. That girl is drowning, Ann, and if you don't stand up to her and get control of the situation right now, she's going to take you under with her." There was a pause before he added, almost as if the idea surprised him, "I'd hate to see that happen."

Ann's lips, her face, her whole body felt stiff—but with fear now, not anger. "What do you mean, she's 'in over her head'? I don't understand."

"I heard her say she'd been up on the mountain, at that religious camp."

"Yes, but I don't see what that has to do with—"

"I warned you about them."

"I know you did, and I—" Ann's voice rose. She glanced at Sunny's door and quickly lowered it to a tense whisper. "I don't believe you. I just don't believe there's any harm in those people. You saw her when she came in—she was *happy*. I haven't seen her look so happy in months.

Months, Niall." Treacherous tears stung her eyes; she brushed them furiously away. "How can I forbid her their friendship? It wouldn't work anyway. You can't choose your children's friends for them, you know, it only makes it worse."

"Maybe not," Niall said in the same tone of voice, "but you can make them less susceptible to what those friends are offering."

"What do you mean?" She held out her hands, pleading with him. "*What* are they offering? It's not like it's drugs, or something. You keep hinting at some kind of danger, but I don't understand what it is!"

Niall opened his mouth, then closed it again. He held up one hand as if conceding the battle and started to turn away. Furious, Ann reached for his arm, found the towel instead and hurled it aside. She caught again at his elbow, neither noticing nor caring that it was like grabbing hold of a tree limb.

"*Tell* me, dammit! What kind of danger? If you know something about those people—"

His hands suddenly closed around her forearms, not hard enough to hurt, but hard enough to remind her of his size and sinewy strength, hard enough to remind her how little she really knew about him. She bit down on her lower lip, holding back words, trying to stifle her anger.

"I *don't* know," Niall said, pushing the words between clenched teeth. "*Yet.* But that's not the point. Don't you understand that? They may be the most benevolent people in the world, but do you want to lose Sunny to them? Would you give your only child up to another family just because they made her *happy?* My God, woman, I may not have any children, but if I did, I know I'd sure as hell fight to keep them with me!"

Ann felt as if the floor were falling out from under her feet, as if she were caught in a vortex, whirling faster and faster, down and down.... She hung on to Niall's forearms for dear life, and when she could speak again, whispered, "Lose Sunny . . . to them? But why would she? How could they— What would they—"

"I told you what they would do—make her feel special . . . important . . . *loved.*"

"But she *is* special and important to me. *I* love her. Why would she—"

"Really? Does she know that?"

Ann sucked in air as if she'd been slapped. It had been a strange sort of quarrel, anyway . . . furious, hurting words never spoken above a whisper. And it was stranger still that the silence in its aftermath should seem so profound when no one had been shouting.

She looked up into eyes as cold, a face as forbidding as an arctic ice floe, and after an eternity whispered, "How *dare* you."

Niall gave a short bark of laughter, a far-from-reassuring sound, more like the warning cough of a hunting tiger. He cupped her chin in his hand, holding it firmly when she would have jerked away. His lips curved in a frosty smile. "How dare I say what I think, or what I know to be true? Believe me, I haven't always. Maybe—" He paused, looking at her with hooded eyes, and said in that same thoughtful, almost puzzling tone he'd used once before, "Maybe because I care about you. Sunny, too, though God only knows why." His voice changed again, became hard and uncompromising. "And sometimes when you care about someone, you have to tell them things you'd rather not—like . . . 'You're grounded.' Understand what I mean?"

Ann lifted her chin, pulled her arms out of his grasp and took one deliberate step away from him. In a voice that trembled with fury she said, "I think you'd better go."

He hesitated only a moment, then nodded and without another word strode past her and out the front door, closing it behind him with precision and restraint.

Ann stood where he'd left her, shaking like a leaf. There were no tears; she felt too cold to cry. Finally, on legs that had turned to blocks of ice, she walked to Sunny's bedroom and opened the door.

* * *

By the time Rankin got to his motel he'd cooled down considerably. His own anger had surprised him. Hers had even more.

He kept remembering the things he'd said to her, the things she'd said to him. The way she'd gone after him, rather like a kitten taking on a Great Dane, he thought, smiling at the memory of her strong little hand clutching his biceps. She hadn't been the least bit daunted, not by his size or his strength, or... or this charming countenance, he thought as he turned on the bathroom light and ran a rueful hand over his stubbled jaws. *Amazing*.

Yeah, amazing. He frowned at his reflection, no longer seeing it, seeing instead what was becoming a familiar vision: a pair of nut-brown eyes with a slightly exotic tilt, a nose with a cluster of freckles on the bridge, a wide, vulnerable mouth. For the life of him he couldn't seem to figure the woman out. He already knew that she was different from any woman he'd ever met, and he kept finding evidence that there was more to soft, sweet Annie Severn than met the eye. For instance, that she had a temper that would make a strong man tread softly! And yet she was scared to death of one unhappy little fifteen-year-old girl. It didn't make sense.

But then, lately it seemed his whole world had stopped making sense. The wars were being fought with different rules now. The enemies were different, the battlegrounds unfamiliar. Even the Wall had come down. God, what beautiful, terrible irony *that* was....

For a moment his eyes blazed back at him out of a dark and terrible face, one he barely recognized. Then in frustration he hauled his shirt up over his head, hurled it into a corner of the room and leaned on his balled up fists. *He* didn't make sense, that was the crux of the matter. He didn't know who he was anymore, didn't even recognize his own thoughts. What was he doing in this town, anyway, running around in the dark playing spy for a local sheriff, pretending he was young again when he knew damn well he wasn't? He was supposed to be in Los Angeles, figuring out what he was going to do with the rest of his life. Right now he should be talking to Joseph Varga about a job, something in corporate security. Industrial espionage. . . .

He shook his head and stared down at the gnarled hands gripping the edge of the sink. Damn it, it wouldn't be the same. It wasn't that the stakes weren't high sometimes. His heart just wouldn't be in it. All his life he'd fought a war he'd been committed to, body and soul. This was someone else's war.

So where was his heart, these days? In the town of *Pinetree?* Why did he give a damn about these people? A week ago he hadn't known they existed. And why was he having such a hard time putting one tiny little woman out of his mind? Since Marta, women to him were a convenience or an inconvenience—and lately more of the latter than the former. There were a few he'd been quite fond of, but the parting when it inevitably came had been final, and for him at least, relatively painless. He'd suffered no qualms of conscience over any of them, because he'd made sure they'd known the rules going in. No permanency, no commitment, no emotional involvement. His heart was off limits. Period.

And it still was; he had no doubts about that. What he couldn't understand was why he wanted this particular woman so badly. It wasn't that she was so beautiful, or so sexy—the waitress at the Buckhorn was probably more his type, generous, uncomplicated, uninhibited. Ann was too intense, too soft, too vulnerable. He'd have to worry about hurting her, in more ways than one.

Of course, on the other hand, as he'd already discovered, she was stronger than she looked. She wasn't intimidated by him, and when he kissed her there hadn't been anything stingy about her response. There had been warmth and passion in it...and above all, honesty. And maybe, he thought, the answer was that simple. She wanted him as much as he wanted her. He was hungry and so was she, and they just naturally kept hitting sparks off each other.

Which was all the more reason to stay the hell away from her until his business here was finished. Right? Simple enough.

Yeah, right.

Leaving the light on in the bathroom, he sat on the foot of the bed to take off his shoes. He felt like he wanted to throw them through a window...or take a bite out of them. He thought he knew how a caged-up tiger felt—frustrated, wound up, sore as a boil. He could discipline his mind, with concentration shut out the images that tormented him—Ann naked and full-length on top of him, soft breasts pillowed on his chest, her cool hands encircling him...stroking him...her mouth— Ah, hell, he could turn off his mind, but he couldn't turn off the fever in his blood, or the ache in his loins.

He thought about going down to the Buckhorn, but the idea didn't really appeal to him. He knew what he wanted, and substitutes, whether liquid or human, weren't worth feeling sorry about in the morning. He'd get over this; he'd had sleepless nights before. Another shower would help—cold, this time.

He stood up, unbuttoned his pants and had the zipper about halfway down when he heard the knock on his door.

Conditioned reflexes had him frozen in a crouch before he'd even identified the sound. An instant later he was flattened against the wall to the right of the door frame, the knife, which until a moment ago had been strapped to his lower leg, concealed in his hand. He listened, breathing suspended, until the knock came again, then slowly, slowly turned the doorknob.

"Niall," came a soft, tentative voice. "I'm sorry to bother you. It's Ann."

Rankin swore and broke out in a cold sweat. He looked at the knife in his hand, looked around for a place to hide it, swore again under his breath and called, "Just a minute," while he put the knife on the edge of the bed and twitched the spread up over it. He gave it one more doubtful look over his shoulder as he pulled the door open.

She was standing there on his doorstep in the silvery light of a bright three-quarter moon, hugging herself, fidgeting in that way people do when they are either freezing or very nervous—and it wasn't that cold a night. She had a jacket on, but it wasn't buttoned, and those blunt-cut wings of hair of hers were tucked every which way into the collar, as if she'd thrown it on in a hurry and without much care. In that light her eyes were only smudges, and her skin had an odd translucence, like porcelain. With a small, unfamiliar shock he realized that she'd been crying.

Oh Lord, he thought as he stood aside to let her in. This is all I need.

"I'm sorry," she said for the second time, punctuating it with a small sniff as she edged through the door. Her voice had a certain tenseness in it, as if she were shaking and trying not to show it. "Were you in bed? I hope I didn't..." Her voice trailed off as her eyes slid across his chest, then down, following the dark line down the middle of his torso to where it ended in the open V of his pants.

Rankin closed the door but didn't move away from her. Instead he stayed right where he was, one hand braced on the wall high above her head. Looming over her like that, he filled his chest with air and let it out slowly. "Ann, what the hell are you doing here?"

She shook her head, freeing some of the hair that was caught in the collar of her coat so that it fell forward into her face. She caught it back with one hand, closed her eyes and whispered, "I guess I shouldn't have come."

"That's right," he rasped. "You shouldn't have."

There was a long silence; he heard the soft, giveaway sound of her swallow. And then she touched him—reached out with one hand and just lightly touched the spot where his chest muscle met his torso. Air hissed between his teeth. He wrapped his fingers around her wrist and jerked her hand away from him as if it had been a red-hot brand, or maybe a cobra. With the hand that gripped hers he backed her roughly up against the wall and held her there.

She didn't say a word. He listened to her quick, shallow breathing and after a while said it again, in a voice like ripping cloth: *"You shouldn't have come."*

She should have been scared to death, but there was no shrinking, no cringing. Her arm was relaxed in his grasp, not fighting him at all. He felt the sexual heat pulsing outward from her body in waves, beckoning to him...sucking him in. And suddenly, without knowing he was going to, he found himself reaching inside the collar of her jacket, pushing his hand under her hair, burrowing his fingers through it, spreading them wide to cradle the back of her head, stroking her cheek with his thumb while he stared down at her wide-open, too-trusting eyes.

"Damn you," he whispered, and kissed her.

Desire enveloped him. It wrapped him in paralyzing sheets, spun him dizzying spirals. It had been too long, eons too long, a lifetime too long. Too long a loneliness in his soul, and something in hers that called like a train whistle in the night. Come with me . . . forget everything and come with me. . . .

He had to pull out of it. Somebody had to, and it wasn't going to be her. He tried...but her mouth was opening, yielding, soft outside, hot inside. Her tongue lay trembling alongside his, sliding over it and under it. Her head was heavy in his hand, jaw thrusting upward, throat arched, reaching for him. Her body rocked with the violence of her heartbeat. . . .

With a hoarse, inarticulate plea he tore his mouth away from hers. He could still feel her shudders. She swallowed once, and then again, and finally uttered one faint, strangled word: "Why?"

His fingers were still caught in her hair; he could feel its silky-soft caress on the back of his hand, mocking the savagery of his emotions. He curled his fingers and listened to her startled gasp with both satisfaction and regret.

"Why?" he repeated on a harsh bark of laughter. "That ought to tell you why, if nothing else. My God, Ann, didn't your mother ever tell you not to go knocking on a strange man's door in the middle of the night?''

''I didn't mean—'' He felt the angle of her head change, her neck muscles tense as she drew a breath. ''I meant, why did you stop... kissing me?''

He stared down at her, angrier than he'd thought he could be, angry with her for being so naive, and with himself for wanting more than anything in the world to pin her to the wall with his body and kiss her again, and go on kissing her until there wasn't anything left to do but make love to her where she stood.

''I don't think you know what you're asking for,'' he said, his voice soft with warning.

''I'm not asking,'' she shot back with unexpected strength. ''I didn't come looking for you, not like that. But I'm not afraid of you, either. I'm not afraid of kissing you, or of... of anything that might happen after that.''

''Yeah?'' His laugh was dry and harsh. Painful. ''Maybe you should be.''

''Why?'' She shrugged and said with maddening simplicity, ''I know you wouldn't hurt me.''

Her assurance infuriated him. He gave her hair another tug and growled, ''You don't know any such thing. How can you? You don't know me.''

''I know that much.'' She moved her head, deliberately testing his hold on her hair, and when he loosened it finally, lifted her chin and shook her hair free in a gesture of pride and confidence.

''You don't know me,'' he repeated, his voice soft, almost caressing, as he let her hair slip like water through his fingers. ''You have no idea who I am, what I've done, what I'm capable of doing.'' He leaned toward her, one hand still holding up the wall above her head, the fingers of the other moving lazily through her hair...around her ear and down the side of her neck... stroking lightly, sensuously, up and down.... ''For instance... did you know that if I increase pressure here—just a little—and hold it, I can cut off the blood supply to your brain? That's all it would take to kill you.''

There was silence, and then in a voice that trembled slightly she said, ''Why are you trying to scare me?''

''Because you're too damn trusting!'' His hand went on stroking her neck, very lightly, very gently, in deliberate contrast with the roughness in his voice, the brutality of his words. ''It's been a long time since I've made love to a woman, Ann. A long time since I've wanted a woman the way I want you. I'm hungry, and my self-control is on a short leash. Lady, you picked a bad time to come knocking on my door.''

There was a long, suspenseful silence, like that which comes between the lightning and the thunder. And then, in a voice so low he could barely hear it, Ann said, ''I didn't come knocking for that.... At least I didn't think I did. But maybe I didn't know. Maybe it's been a long time for me, too. Did you ever think of that? Just maybe... I'm hungry too.''

There was another silence, while Rankin closed his eyes and clenched his jaws so tightly he thought his teeth might shatter, wondering if he pushed hard enough on that wall he could manage to bring the whole damn building down on top of them. His body was a brush fire and he was fast running out of the energy and resolve he needed to fight it. ''Ann,'' he said finally in a harsh, guttural voice, ''do you have any idea what you're talking about?''

''Of course,'' she said, her own voice more confident now. ''I'm a grown-up woman, not a child.''

''You're one kind of woman,'' he agreed, forcing words between his teeth. ''Not the kind of woman to crawl into a stranger's bed, knowing he's got nothing to give her—no nice words, no promises, no tomorrows—nothing but a warm body and maybe a way to stop the loneliness for a little while....'' But he was touching her again, his palm on her throat, his thumb and fingers stroking almost idly, back and forth along her jaw. And she was touching him. Not idly, trembling slightly. He felt her hand on his torso. Not cool, now, but warm . . . honey warm.

"You don't know what kind of woman I am," she whispered.

He leaned forward slowly, deliberately, pushing against her hand, forcing it back, finally trapping it between his hard, naked body and her soft breasts.

"Just as long as you know the rules." The last word was a half-groan, stifled in her open, waiting mouth.

The rules of what? I don't even know the game!

The clarity of the thought surprised Ann. She was dizzy, her body a conflagration, her heart a runaway freight train, but it was only her body that was out of control. Her mind seemed perfectly capable of rational thought. She wasn't going to be able to justify this by saying she'd "lost her head." She knew exactly what she was doing.

And as far as she was concerned, she didn't intend to justify it at all. Why should she need to? She hadn't slept with a man since Mark's death—hadn't met anyone she'd wanted to go to bed with, though there had been opportunities. That didn't exactly make her promiscuous, did it? But lately, with all her problems with Sunny, she'd been feeling so helpless, so *alone*. And tonight—tonight was just the last straw. She needed someone to cling to, someone with broad shoulders and strong arms to hold her. She *needed* someone, that was all.

Yes, that clear-thinking mind of hers questioned, *but why* this *particular man . . . this stranger?*

Because she needed someone, and Niall was there, and maybe something in her had sensed the need in him, too. It was just a matter of timing, she answered herself. He happened to be there at the right moment, that was all.

Yes, that clear-thinking mind of hers persisted, *but what if that's not true? What if it is only* this *man that you need? What will you do when he moves on to wherever it is he belongs?*

Don't think. Don't think about that, don't think about anything. Just feel . . . and forget.

She felt hot. She had too many layers of clothing on. Niall apparently thought so, too, because he brought his arm down and in one swift, sure motion shucked her jacket off and hurled it out of the way. The hand on her throat moved down, briefly kneaded her breast through her sweater, then hauled impatiently at the heavy fabric, pushed it up and found the yielding softness underneath.

His hands were rough and hot and greedy; her skin was hotter and even more eager. Her breasts ached to fill his hands. Her nipples were so tender that when he touched them through her bra she gasped and cried out. He answered her by rubbing them harder, by driving his tongue deep, deep into her mouth, filling it and sealing it with his, wringing tiny helpless whimpers from her with the rhythmic thrusts of his tongue and the insistent pressure of his fingers, until her world spun and darkened and her knees buckled....

She surfaced in Niall's lap. Somehow he was sitting on the foot of the bed, supporting her with one arm as she lay across his knees, with her sweater bunched around her neck, her fingers digging into his back, and her heart banging so wildly against her rib cage that she could hardly breathe. His heart was banging, too. She could hear it, feel it, because her head was pressed against his chest; one big hand held it there while the other lay on her stomach, fingers spread wide, stroking softly, gently now, quieting them both down.

She turned her face into his chest and found the dark shadowed places, the unfamiliar texture of hair. She found it fascinating. Mark hadn't had any hair on his—

Don't think.

She burrowed her face and fingers through it, liking the way it felt, liking the just-showered, fresh-sweat smell of him. She opened her mouth and tasted him, nipping gently with her teeth, laving his skin with her tongue, finding the flat, smooth nipple and teasing it until his fingers curled spasmodically on her belly, closed roughly on her hip and buttock and lifted her up to meet his hot, hungry mouth again.

Oh God, she thought, this feels so good. It's been so long....

Don't think.

Eight

Ann....

Rankin spread his fingers across her bare stomach, feeling nerves jump and tremble under skin as soft and smooth as silk, and thought about the things he'd just said to her. The memories didn't make him feel good, but they didn't cool the fires inside him, either.

In any case it was all true, he told himself, feeling no pride in the fact. I tried to warn her. At least she knows the score going in.

Except that he knew she didn't, not really. She thought she did, but it was only the need talking. Making love to her was still wrong, at least under the circumstances. But he knew he was going to anyway, unless she had the good sense to stop him. His own need was so great that he was going to give in to it. He was going to turn off his mind and his conscience and take everything she had to give him, and give her back what he could, which wasn't saying much. She deserved more.

He knew that what he ought to do was stop kissing her right now, set her feet back on the floor and tell her to put on her coat and go home. What he did instead was kiss her all the more. He kissed her deeply, as if he could bury himself, lose himself in her. He kissed her hungrily, as if he really were starving and couldn't ever get enough. And then . . . He slipped searching fingers under the waistband of her pants, found the button, then the zipper, and eased it slowly down.

Ann, if you're going to stop me, for God's sake, do it now, he cried silently.

What she did instead was turn toward him, pushing against his hand in silent invitation, her breathing quick and shallow with suspense. He pushed his hand under nylon and elastic and moved it back and forth over her hip and belly, working it farther down. She shifted her legs, making it easier for him. He slid his fingers into the hot, damp place between her thighs. She shuddered. Her belly heaved beneath his hand; her thighs trembled.

From somewhere, God only knew where, he found the strength to stop. He held her, just held her like that, her body so soft and light in his arms, the softest and most vulnerable part of her warmly housed in his hand. He could feel her pulse there. His own pulse almost strangled him, but somehow he managed to bring his lips close to her ear and whisper, "Ann, I don't have anything. I have no way of protecting you."

"It's all right." Her voice was low and urgent, pouring warmth into the hollow of his neck. "I'm still on the Pill. I tried to go off after Mark died, but my—"

"*Don't*. You don't have to tell me. I don't want to know."

"But it's not—"

"No—don't talk. If you're covered, that's all I need to know." No, don't talk . . . please, not now. Talking meant thinking and if he had to think about her he'd remember who she was and who he was, and all the reasons why he'd sworn he wasn't going to do what he was about to do.

So to keep her from talking he kissed her again, kissed her mouth hard and deep until she had no more breath, kissed her with a kind of fever, all over her face, her eyelids, lips and throat, until her breathing grew labored and harsh, and her heartbeat rebounded against *his* ribs. Then he murmured something guttural and inarticulate and tugged her pants over her hips and all the way down. They hung up momentarily on her shoes; he heard a soft thump as one hit the floor.

When she was as naked as he needed her to be, he lifted and resettled her, telling her with muttered words and urgent hands what he wanted of her, so that she was astride him, now, with her arms locked around his neck.

"Hold on," he whispered, and stood up. She laughed and clung to him, her face buried in the hollow of his neck, trembling, trusting....

He'd never felt such urgency. The need to be inside her was primitive and unreasoning, reckless and single-minded, all the things he was not, and had never thought he could be. He knew that her hunger was as great as his own, that she was allowing herself no more opportunity for clear thinking than he was. What was driving him—and perhaps her, too—was the fear that at any moment one or the other of them would wake up and common sense and reason return, and the moment, *this* moment would be lost forever.

And so he wasted no time on unnecessary preparations. In some part of his mind he was sorry that he couldn't undress her little by little, enjoying the sight of her naked and getting to know her body, taking pleasure in her pleasure as he touched her in all the ways he knew, letting the excitement in his own body slowly build while he watched her skin turn dusky with desire, felt her body heat and swell in his mouth and hands, until he knew she was ready and so was he, and that the merging would be easy and the explosion sweet.

But not now. There was no time for that now. When he sat down with her again he was naked, hot and hard, and he hoped to God she was ready.

She knew exactly what he wanted. She locked her legs around him and pulled herself against him, belly to belly. He gripped her buttocks tightly and drove a gasp from her lungs with a swift, deep penetration. Pleasure enveloped him, so sweet and intense it was almost pain. Holding her there, he put his head back and groaned....

Ann held him with every ounce of strength she had, her body shaking, on the verge of sobs. She held him not for her own sake but for his, because with a woman's instinct she knew that he was a man in danger of falling apart, and that only she could hold him together. She felt the power in his surging body and straining muscles, and the vulnerability and pain inside him. She didn't understand it, but the whys didn't matter; he was a man in pain, and for reasons she wouldn't allow herself to think about, that was all that mattered. She held him with a fierce and primitive protectiveness while his body arched and convulsed, opening herself to him without reserve, making herself a receptacle for his pent-up anguish, even as she used her own body's inner contractions to encourage and nourish his physical release. And when it was over and they clung together, rocking with the rhythms of slowing heartbeats, their bodies slippery with cooling sweat, she found that her face was wet, too. With tears.

For a long time neither of them moved, neither of them spoke. Then Niall eased his hold on her bottom, gently unhooked her legs and lay back, pulling her with him and wrapping her in the warm, protective circle of his arms. Ann snuggled into the nest he offered without question or hesitation. She lay as still as she could, hoping he hadn't noticed her tears, hoping she wouldn't have to explain them. She dared not try, even to herself.

Don't think, she told herself.

But the time was coming, the time for thinking...and talking. She dreaded that moment, because Niall's words had frightened her. Because her own thoughts couldn't be put into words, and if they could have, they would have frightened her even more.

The moment was inevitable, but she could control its direction and tone, at least, by initiating it herself. So she made a soft, throat-clearing sound and said lightly, "I have a question."

"Ask."

His hands were moving up and down her back, his touch as delicate as a butterfly's, as light as down. She thought about the way they looked—scarred and rough, the fingers blunt and slightly crooked, hands that had endured unknown horrors, and maybe committed a few. The exquisite gentleness of his touch and the image of those hard, brown hands on her naked skin produced an odd collision of senses. She shivered and drew her leg up, restless now, certain burgeoning sensations in her body reminding her that her own release had been emotional rather than physical.

Twelve years of celibacy had made her fairly adept at squelching her body's demands. Willing herself to stillness, she murmured, "I was just wondering what you'd have done if I hadn't been on the Pill."

"Huh?" She felt his chest jerk with ironic laughter.

"Would you have called it off?"

"*Hell* no."

"What, then?"

He raised his head and looked at her. She wondered how blue eyes could have so much heat in them. "What would I have done? I'd have gotten creative..."

He lay back again, his laughter soft...sultry. In spite of all her willpower, Ann began to tremble. Niall's hand had begun its gentle stroking again, down over her buttock and along the back of her drawn-up thigh. And then his arms suddenly tightened; he shifted her slightly and reached under her, searching for her hot, humid places, sliding his fingers between her still swollen, still damp folds.

Sensation shot through her, bright and sharp as pain, driving the breath from her. His fingers opened her, penetrated her, sought and found her most vulnerable and sensitive places; his fingers touched her in ways she'd never imagined—now a silken, erotic glide, now an electrifying pressure deep inside. In seconds she was panting...then sobbing, her body out of control. She cried out, "No—please—" Then she was clinging to him, exhilarated and terrified, in the grip of spasms she feared would stop her heart.

And finally, as she lay stunned upon his chest, she heard him say softly, "Like that."

It was a long time before she wanted to try to move again...or think...or talk. But she did, finally, turning her hot face into the damp hair beneath her cheek and hiding it there, inexplicably embarrassed.

"I didn't think you knew," she said in a muffled voice.

His chuckle was dry, and held a note of regret. "I guess I deserve that. I wasn't exactly—how shall I put it—*sensitive* to your needs."

Ann was silent for a long time. Her hand uncurled on his chest; her fingers spread wide, burrowing through his hair in a way that was both sensual and wondering. "Maybe," she said softly, "you don't know what my needs are."

"Maybe." She felt his belly tense as he lifted his head to look at her. "It's possible I don't." He relaxed again and lay back, stroking her hair with one hand. "Tell me what they are, little one." His voice was soft and slightly furry. "You said when you came here it wasn't for this. What did you come for?"

"It's funny...."

"What is?"

His hand... The stroking was so soothing. She wanted to stay like this forever, in the warm cocoon of his arms, rising and falling with his breathing like a boat rocking on a gentle swell.

"Mmm," she murmured, squirming a little, making an effort to think. "I thought I knew what I wanted when I came here. I was upset.... After you left I went into Sunny's room to talk to her, but she was asleep. *Really* asleep, if you can believe it. Here I was so angry with her... but when I looked at her, when I saw her face—"

She stopped and took a deep breath. Niall's hand was still now, just holding her. She drew strength from it, and after a moment went on, but in a whisper. "I felt...this love for her—my little girl. I felt like I was going to explode with it, you know? And...suddenly I knew you were right. That I don't tell her. I *can't* tell her. Niall, I'm so afraid of losing her—I don't know what I'd do if I lost her....

"I lost Mark. I tried so hard to stop it. I loved him so much, and then I felt him slipping away from me.... I guess I thought if I loved him enough I could keep it from happening. I hung on with everything I had...nagged him every day about getting help, seeing a doctor—anything. I think it made it worse. I think I drove him away with my nagging...my worrying. Maybe if I'd given him more space...more time...."

"So that's what you're trying to give Sunny? Space...time?"

"She's like Mark in so many ways. It frightens me." She drew a quick little breath, more like a sniff. "Anyway, I was upset, and I wanted to see you, to tell you. I thought I wanted to tell you that you were right about Sunny. To apologize for...for the way I acted. But I think what I really wanted was..."

"Tell me." His lips were brushing her hair. The words spread a pool of warmth over her scalp and down, all through her. "Tell me what you wanted."

"I just wanted...to be *held*. I wanted to feel your arms around me, even if it was only for one night. Even if I never saw you again. I wanted you to hold me."

His arms tightened, then, wrapped around and enfolded her. She felt the prickly rasp of his jaw against her temple. "I can give you that," he whispered roughly. "I'll hold you tonight...for as long as you want to stay. That much I promise you."

She settled on his chest again with a soft, painful little chuckle, while Rankin stared into the gray darkness above her head, his eyes dry and burning, his chest and throat tight with the pressure of an unfamiliar pain. He couldn't understand it. He'd never felt like this before, not in the hell-years in East Germany, thinking of Marta, dreaming of revenge, not in the lonely years after that, playing the deadly cat-and-mouse games, relying only on himself and his ability to think without emotions, trusting *no one*.

Yet here he was now with a woman naked in his arms, a woman he'd thought about holding like this, a woman he'd just made love to... a scrap of a woman, soft and sweet as flower petals and not much heavier... and he felt as if she were the only thing keeping him from exploding. He wondered if she knew he was holding her so tightly because he feared that if he let go of her he might take off like a malfunctioning rocket.

"Niall?" It was a soft, sleepy sigh.

"Hmm?"

"Have you ever loved someone... so much?"

"Once," he said after a moment. "A long time ago."

"A woman?"

"Yes."

"Where is she now?"

"Dead." Before she could respond to that, he slipped his fingers under her chin, turned her face up and found her mouth with his.

He kissed her differently this time, the way he'd wanted to do in the first place, long and languid and slow...sultry as a summer night in Naples. Her hand rode the swells and hollows of his chest and neck and came to rest on his jaw, her fingers stroking through the stubble to trace its harsh angles and planes.

His own hands had a smoother journey. From her shoulders he let them glide slowly down, taking their sweet time, exploring with all the sensual pleasure he had in him, savoring the softness of her skin, the gentle indentations of her spine, the tender muscles in her back, coming together at the narrow span of waist, then blossoming over the lush feminine swell of hips and bottom....

Under his caress she moved like a cat, sinuously, caressing him at the same time with her body. He stroked and petted her, writhing with her, the pace as slow and unhurried as a blues melody. When the time seemed right, he raised her up and brought her breasts to his mouth, nipped and teased with lips and tongue until the nipples grew hard and her breathing sharpened, then sucked them deep into his mouth while she arched her back and moaned.

And then he raised her higher, coaxing her past her shyness with love words and firm hands. He spread her and kissed her inner thighs and the honey-damp curls at their juncture, slipped his tongue between her soft folds, pleasuring her, bringing her to the precipice time and time again, until she begged him, sobbing and trembling, "Please. Oh God, no more... I *can't*...."

So once more he lifted her, settled her. Her wet, pulsing body embraced his hot flesh as an oasis welcomes a thirsty soul, and even as he poured himself into her with a shuddering, driving force that left him utterly drained, in a strange way he also felt... nourished.

Later, fighting his way through layers of tiredness and unprecedented contentment, Rankin stirred experimentally and managed to murmur, "Are you cold?"

He thought she must be asleep, but after a moment she drew an uneven breath and said softly but clearly, "Yes, a little. But I don't want to move."

His chuckle was rueful. "Neither do I, but I think...I'm going to have to. Here—"

When he eased her off him and onto the mattress she winced and said, "Ouch!"

Tenderness assailed him. He kissed her and pulled the bedspread over her, said gently, "Stay there, I'll bring you something," and went into the bathroom, feeling just a touch of remorse.

When he came out, she was sitting up in the middle of the bed with the spread wrapped around her Indian-style. Even in the semidarkness he could see the quizzical expression on her face. And the one bare arm that reached toward him from out of the folds of the bedspread, as if in supplication. On its upturned palm lay his knife.

"It was under the bedspread," she said in an odd, faraway voice. "It poked me."

Niall flicked on the lamp on the dresser. Fascinated, yet protected by a strange detachment, Ann watched the play of emotions across his face. They went quickly—alarm, concern, a touch of anger, even, as unlikely as it seemed, embarrassment—and then his features settled into a mask of ice and shadows, utterly devoid of expression. He took the knife from her without comment, hefted it once and casually added it to the miscellaneous litter on the dresser.

"It didn't hurt you, did it?" he asked remotely, his back to her.

"N-no." The stammer appalled her. She prayed he wouldn't notice.

He came and sat on the edge of the bed, the towel he'd brought for her casually draped across his lap. Unwillingly drawn to his body, Ann's eyes took note of what they'd missed in the darkness—the small but unmistakable marks of violence.

"You're frightened." His voice was flat and without apology.

Her first instinct was to deny it. Then she began to feel indignant. Frightened? To make love with a stranger and then find a knife in his bed? Of course she was frightened. She *should* be frightened. And yet...

"No," she said, frowning, "I'm confused."

The icy mask melted, taking the remoteness with it. His smile was wry, but it touched his eyes. "I told you, you don't know me."

"I want to," she whispered. "Tell me."

"I can't. I'm sorry." He sounded sad.

Ann felt a lump in her throat, a heaviness in her chest. "You've used that knife, haven't you?" she persisted, touching a long thin scar on his ribs.

"Oh yes." He gave a dry, ironic chuckle. "And vice versa, as you can see." He took her hand and enfolding it in both of his, carried it to his lips. "So you see now why I warned you? You wanted to be held. Perhaps you should find gentler arms."

Unexpected and unexplainable tears rushed to the backs of her eyes, making it impossible for her to speak. Instead she put her free hand over his clasped ones and drew them to her; holding them in her lap she began to caress them with her fingertips, exploring the hard ridges of bone and sinew, the thin ropes of scar tissue below the wrists.

Presently, looking only at his hands, she was able to whisper, "Niall, I have to ask you something."

"Ask. I'll answer if I can."

"The woman you loved—how did she die?"

He hesitated for only a moment, then said flatly, "She was shot."

"Who shot her?" Ann swallowed, then pushed the words past the weight in her chest. "Did you?"

His voice was very soft. "Why would you think so?"

She drew a deep, trembling breath. "There was... something in your voice when you mentioned her. A coldness. It scared me." Still not looking at his face, still stroking his battered hands, she persisted, "Did you?"

"No." She heard the sigh of his exhalation. "Though I may have had a hand in it. She...got caught in the cross fire of a war without rules." He was silent for a moment, and when he spoke again his voice was even softer, almost musing. "There was a time when I wanted to kill her, more than anything in the world. I think it may have been the only thing keeping me alive, at the time."

Ann's throat was so tight, so raw, she could barely utter the single word, *"Why?"*

"She betrayed me," Niall said, his voice barren and cold. "She betrayed all of us. Several died. Others, including myself, fared worse. Innocent people...children... suffered. Because I trusted her." He repeated it in a harsh, bitter whisper. "I trusted her...."

In the awful silence that followed, a tear began a long, cool slide toward the end of Ann's nose. Before she could catch it, it fell with an audible splash onto the back of Niall's hand. For one tense moment they both stared at it. Then Ann sniffed and Niall laughed softly. He turned his hands and closed them gently around her wrists.

"Why are you crying, little one?" His thumbs traced the fragile tendons on the inside of her wrists. "It was a long time ago. It doesn't matter anymore."

"If it doesn't matter, then tell me about it." Her chin had a staunch, uncompromising look.

Annie's tougher than she looks. Rankin remembered those words as he stared down at the slender wrists in his hands...the skin so soft and smooth, with a tracing of blue veins and a few—just a few—widely scattered freckles. Annie's tough....

He took a deep breath and heard himself say, "Her name was Marta. I was just eighteen when I met her. I was involved with a group...never mind the name. We were digging a tunnel under the Wall."

"The *Berlin* Wall?"

"Yes. I met Marta in East Berlin. She said she wanted to escape. So my friends and I arranged it. The details don't matter—it was daring and foolish and we were lucky—it worked. Then she told me she had family in East Berlin, and she wanted to try to get them out as well. By this time I was completely in love with her. I was also very young, and very naive. In any cause, I believed her. I brought her to our group."

"And she betrayed you," Ann prompted when he stopped.

"Yes," Rankin said on a long exhalation. "She betrayed us. Fortunately, the rest of the group was not as trusting—or besotted—as I. Only a small handful of us knew where the tunnel entrances were. All others—the escapees, for their own protection as well as ours—were taken to the tunnel blindfolded. Marta brought the secret police to the meeting place on the East Berlin side. Several of our group were killed. The others were arrested, along with those who had come hoping only to escape...families with small children...old people. I never knew what happened to them.''

"What happened to *you?*" He felt her hands tighten on his forearms. "*Tell* me."

"Me? I was one of those arrested." His lips twisted. "For a long time they thought they would persuade us to tell them where the tunnel was."

"Your hands...." Her voice was hushed, horrified.

"My hands...yes." He laughed without amusement. "They finally gave up. Later I found out that no one ever told them. The others who were arrested with me all died, but I...for some reason, I survived. Eventually, I escaped. But in the meantime, I had learned a good many valuable lessons—how to kill, for example. Silently and efficiently. Most of all, however, I learned how to survive. I learned that in the game of survival anything goes...that emotions are liabilities, and nothing is ever what it seems. That to trust *anyone* is a mistake. And I assure you that I did not make any more mistakes...."

The room was very quiet, except for the growl of a truck going by on the highway. Ann's head was bowed, the fine, silken wings of her hair falling like a curtain across her face. When Rankin put his fingers under her chin and gently nudged it upward, he wasn't surprised to see the sheen of tears.

He laughed softly. "And *now,* little one? Now will you tell me why you are crying?"

"I'm crying for you, of course," she said steadily, almost angrily. "Because you've been so hurt. Because—"

His hand cradled her cheek; his smile was tender. "But there's no reason to cry for me. I have no feelings, so I can't be hurt. I have no heart, so I will never have it broken. I do not trust, so I will never know betrayal. I have no emotions at all—I only pretend. So you see—" he shrugged and gently brushed tears from her cheek "—you have nothing at all to cry about."

...But if he had no heart, what was this that lay in his chest like a lump of molten rock? If he had no feelings, why this ache that encompassed him from his face right down to his toes? And if he didn't trust anyone, why had he just told this woman things he'd never told another soul? Supposedly devoid of emotions, why was he feeling something now that was akin to panic?

The feeling grew the longer he looked at Ann, at that soft mouth, and those tear-blurred eyes of hers—big and brown and luminous as a fawn's. Opposing feelings raced through him like converging locomotives. Marta had had innocent eyes, too. They had been black and beguiling—and deceptive—as moonlight on quiet water....

Rankin stood up rather too abruptly, turning his back to the bed while he knotted the towel around his hips. His head swam with fatigue.

"Where are you going?" Ann asked quietly.

He frowned at her over his shoulder. "To put some clothes on. I'll take you home."

She looked at the digital clock on the radio beside the bed, then back at him. Her chin was up, in that stubborn way he was beginning to recognize. "You promised me tonight."

One eyebrow shot upward; he gave a dry, disbelieving snort. "You still want me to hold you? I thought you were afraid."

"I'm not afraid." She let the bedspread fall. "And I still want you to hold me." Her voice was soft and slightly thickened. "Just for tonight..."

Nine

Rankin slept the clock around. It was hunger that woke him, finally—woke him and dragged him kicking and clawing through the suffocating layers of exhaustion that encased him like a mummy's wrappings. And he felt as though he'd been lying around in a tomb for a couple of thousand years, he thought in disgust as he fumbled his way to the bathroom. He really was getting too old for this sort of thing.

He turned on the light and gave his blurry reflection in the mirror a critical once-over, thinking as he surveyed his bearded jaws and bloodshot eyes that it probably wouldn't be a good idea to try to shave in this condition; he'd only cut his own throat. On the other hand he was starving, and if he went into the Buckhorn looking like this he'd likely scare the waitress to death.

God, it had been a long time since he'd felt like this in the morning! Or was it morning? The light didn't feel right, somehow. He just wished he could remember....

Cigarettes. He'd decided to hell with quitting—*that* much he remembered. He was going to buy himself a pack first thing. They'd have them at the Buckhorn.

His eyes suddenly narrowed. His fingers skimmed the stubble on his chin, moved on down his throat and stopped at the small, dusky red mark just above his collarbone. Ann's mark.

Ann. He closed his eyes and gripped the edge of the sink, leaning on his hands for support while the strength ran out of his muscles like water through a sieve.

He remembered.

Ann slept as late as she could on Saturday morning, which was until Sunny got up and started banging around in the kitchen making herself breakfast. It would be French toast. Sunny always wanted French toast or waffles on Saturday, she didn't have the patience for waffles.

Ann was feeling pretty hungry herself. Thinking about the reasons for that made her squirm and stretch in delicious languor; it had been a long time since she'd felt like this in the morning. Physically, anyway. Her emotions were another matter.

You still want me to hold you?

She could still see him standing there, one eyebrow raised in that way he had, his hair falling rakishly over his forehead, a ridiculously inadequate motel towel wrapped around his hips...no longer the elegant stranger who'd come to her door with Sunny that terrible night, or even the lean and dangerous hunter she'd walked in on unexpectedly in Bill's office, but a flesh-and-blood, not-quite-ordinary, but very human man. A strong man, yes; in many ways a hard man, a man from a world she could never know, with a past she couldn't begin to understand. A tired man, rumpled and unshaven, a man she'd just made love with.

I'm not afraid... and I still want you to hold me.

A lonely and vulnerable man...a man who needed her.

As she'd felt his cool, hard body come against hers, and settled with a sigh into the comforting circle of his arms, it had occurred to her to wonder exactly who was holding whom.

Just for tonight....

She thought she must have dreamed about the panther as she lay half-dozing in Niall's arms, waiting for the first light of morning, knowing that when it came she would have to tear herself away from him and slip through the cold streets to her own house, her own bed. Or maybe she'd just been thinking about the man whose heartbeat knocked so strongly against her ear, the man who'd told her he had no heart. When he'd said that, she'd felt as if her own heart were breaking. And lying there beside him in the gray dawn, gently rocked by the slow, even rhythm of his breathing, she'd cried once more for the man who'd said he'd never trust again.

But he'd trusted her.

The realization burst upon her, soft and radiant as a desert sunrise. She knew the things he'd told her hadn't come easily; she was certain he wasn't in the habit of talking about himself—to anyone. But he'd talked to her. Maybe it had been the time and place. Maybe he'd been lonely, or tired, and she'd caught him at a weak moment. But it didn't matter. He might be gone tomorrow, but wherever he went he had left a part of himself here...with her.

He trusted *her.*

B.J. was on the breakfast shift, so there was a different waitress at the Buckhorn. According to the tag on her uniform pocket, her name was Terry. She was short and generously built, had thick, curly black hair and a nice smile, and brown eyes that reminded Rankin of Ann's. Of course, everything lately reminded him of Ann.

The waitress's tentative flirting made Rankin restless. Memories of Ann and the night—morning?—just past were still vivid in his mind and painful as a freshly stubbed toe.

For the life of him, he couldn't understand how he could have let things go so far. It was unforgivable. He who was known for his cold, calculating mind, his ability to make decisions without emotions—he'd known what was right and had made his decision accordingly, and then watched his carefully arrived-at resolutions go up in smoke.

Smoke. Ah yes....

He bought the cigarettes when he paid his check. While the waitress was ringing up his bill and making change, he found himself staring at the way her full breasts strained the buttons of her uniform. He thought of Ann, and the way her breasts had felt...against his chest, in his hands, in his mouth. Desire whipped through him with such violence that for a moment he felt dizzy.

The waitress handed him his change and sang, "There you go, sir, have a nice evening!" He shoved the cigarettes into his jacket pocket and pushed blindly through the door and into the cool desert night.

Out on the sidewalk he tore the pack open, tapped out a cigarette and stuck it in his mouth, then reached in his pocket for his lighter. And remembered he no longer had one. He took one step back toward the Buckhorn, where, he was certain, he would find matches. Then stopped and took the cigarette out of his mouth and hurled it into the street.

Damn this town! He'd swear it was doing something to his willpower. Ann...cigarettes. His resolve had about as much effect against one as the other.

He wanted to see Ann again. And he knew he could not. He must not.

More than he'd wanted anything in years, he wanted to walk straight to Ann's house, knock on her door and haul her into his arms. He wanted to make love to her tonight, and every night for the foreseeable future. But...it was the unforeseeable future that made that impossible. Because, while she'd only asked him for one night, he knew she wasn't the kind of woman to be content with that. She was a settler, the kind of woman who stayed in one place and with one man for a lifetime, and he couldn't give her that. All he could give her was heartache.

Willpower. Rankin took the pack of cigarettes out of his pocket and laid it on top of the newspaper rack in front of the Buckhorn, where, he expected, it was going to make some lucky smoker's evening. Then he walked back to the Whispering Pines Motel, got in his car, pulled out onto the highway and headed south, out of town.

It would be best for everyone concerned, he thought as the chamber of commerce's Welcome to Pinetree sign retreated in his rearview mirror, if he just kept driving until he got to Los Angeles. Ann would forget him soon enough. She'd find some nice guy and get married again. And Sunny...well, the world was full of mixed-up kids like her, and most of them managed to grow up in spite of everything. In any case, she wasn't his concern.

Several miles outside of town he passed a sign that said, "Quarry, 1 mile." It had an arrow pointing to the right, up a narrow dirt road. He wondered if it was the same quarry where twelve years or so ago, Mark Severn, local hero and ex-basketball star, had shot himself and a truck stop waitress. He wondered if local teenagers still went there to park and make love....

A little farther on he came to another dirt road heading off to the left. It had no sign at all. He turned onto it and in a few minutes found himself out in the middle of nowhere, with nothing around him but desert and nothing above him but stars. He turned off the motor and headlights and got out of the car. The wind was blowing, as it always seemed to do in the desert, making him wish he had on a warmer coat. Other than that, it was a good place for thinking.

He thought about leaving Pinetree. He could do it right now, tonight, and probably ought to. But he'd promised Bill he'd find out what was going on in that compound up there in the mountains, and he didn't like to go back on a promise. That infrared camera he'd had sent from Washington wouldn't be here until tomorrow at the earliest, and maybe not until Monday, and there wasn't much more he could do without it. So for the next few days, at least, he was stuck here.

He thought about staying in Pinetree. Permanently. He hadn't intended to, but the idea had been there, knocking on the windows of his mind, trying to get his attention, and he couldn't keep ignoring it. Especially out here in the middle of nowhere, with nothing but the sigh of the wind to drown it out.

He thought about Ann's house, with the family photos on the walls, the ruffled curtains and the African violet on the windowsill. He thought about quiet streets that smelled of lilacs, where people called and waved to each other, and stopped for a while to talk.

Where, in a town like that, was there a place for him—a burned-out, disillusioned secret agent with no more wars to fight?

And what about him? Could he learn to live without the danger, the challenge of the game? To accept people at face value, to stop jumping at shadows. To trust. To love again.

Rankin listened, hoping for answers. He heard only the wind.

Niall was gone again. Ann got that piece of gossip from Allie Henshaw Sunday morning after church. According to Allie, a package had come for Mr. Rankin that morning, by special messenger. "On a Sunday morning—can you believe it?" And when Mr. Rankin had come to the office to pick it up, he'd been dressed in rugged clothes, like he was going up to the mountains. "And he don't look like the fishin' type, to me."

Allie finished by rolling her eyes and smacking her lips. "That is the sexiest man I ever saw in a pair of hiking boots, that's all I can say!" she said. Which made everybody laugh, because as everyone knew, Allie and her husband Ed were so sweet on each other it would give a person cavities just to be in the same room with them. Allie was one of those women people always said would be "so beautiful if she'd only lose some weight.'' Ann had always thought it was kind of nice that Ed Henshaw thought she was beautiful just the way she was.

In any case, Allie told her, Mr. Rankin had left all his things and asked Ed to hold the room for him for a few days. "Well, Ed told him, I guess it's your money!'' Then he'd taken his mysterious package and driven off in his car.

Allie nudged Ann in the ribs. "What do you suppose he's up to?''

Ann shrugged and tried not to look guilty. She didn't have any idea how much Allie knew or suspected about her visit to Niall's room in the wee hours of Saturday morning, but it was obvious Allie had an idea she could supply some missing pieces to the puzzle. Which of course she could, but wasn't about to do. Not in a million years.

But if Ann didn't have anything to offer on the subject of the mysterious stranger in town, there were plenty of others who did—most of it about as farfetched as a B movie plot.

Lillian Saunders, who taught third grade, and whose husband was the local insurance agent, suggested he might be a government geologist, or one of those people who study volcanoes, and that the package could be one of those machines for monitoring earth movement. After all, Lil said, everyone was always saying Mammoth Mountain up north of Bishop was going to be the next Mount Saint Helens; maybe it was getting ready to blow and they didn't want anyone to know about it and start a panic!

Someone thought he might be a prospector, and that the package contained some sort of new-fangled ore detector.

"No,'' Allie said, flatly dismissing that with a shake of her head. "Did you ever see a prospector who dressed like that? I swear, even in outdoor clothes, there's just something... I don't know... *different* about him.''

"It's because he doesn't wear jeans,'' Terry, the evening waitress from the Buckhorn, said with a wistful note in her voice. "Everybody around here wears jeans, all the time.''

"Well," said Allie, widening her eyes with delicious excitement, "here's what *I* think. I think he's one of those foreign movie or TV producers, and he's scouting for locations, or something. Ed thinks I'm out of my mind, but it would sure explain the accent, and the way he dresses, and you know how those movie people are about money! And I'll bet that package was a camera of some— What did you say, Ann?"

"Nothing," she said, coughing to cover an involuntary start, because she'd just remembered what Niall had said to Bill as he was leaving his office Friday night, something about a camera and Monday.

"Well, anyway, that's my theory," Allie concluded, just as Patty Clemson walked up with Will. "What do you think, Patty? My God, Will, I think you grow another foot everytime I see you! Patty, we've decided they're gettin' ready to make another movie around here. Does Bill know anything about that?"

As Patty was swallowed up by the gossipers, Will sidled over to Ann. "Sunny around?" he mumbled, looking unhappy enough to kick something.

"She should be here somewhere." Ann was craning her neck to see through the crowd of socializing churchgoers when Sunny came running up. She stopped as if she'd hit a wall the minute she saw Will, then came on, her chin and her color both high. It was a look Ann recognized. Pure bravado.

"Hi, Mom," she said, all buoyant, breathless innocence, studiously ignoring Will. "Can I go to my friends' house? I *promise* I won't be late this time. Can I, *please?*"

"Well..." Ann said uncertainly, torn between her recent resolve and the happy sparkle in her daughter's eyes. She'd meant to ground Sunny after Friday's episode, but she really did seem genuinely contrite about that.... "What about homework? And have you fed Sarge?"

"I did all my homework yesterday. And Sarge still has plenty of food. I checked this morning before we left for church. So can I go? Please?"

"All right," Ann capitulated with a sigh. "But be sure and be home before dark."

"I *will*, I promise. Thanks, Mom. Bye!" She was already gone before Ann could respond.

"I can't believe she's going around with those people," Will muttered, angrily kicking the ground. "I can't believe you *let* her. What's with her lately, anyway? She won't even talk to me."

"I've been wondering about that," Ann said. "Did you two have a fight or something?"

"Not a fight exactly. More of a misunderstanding, I guess you could say."

The glance he threw her as he went on digging a hole in the church parking lot with his tennis shoe was so full of misery and frustration that Ann tactfully steered him to a more private spot and murmured, "Maybe you ought to tell me what happened, Will. I know she's been pretty upset about something."

He nodded. "Yeah, but if she'd just let me explain...."
He fidgeted a while longer, then looked at Ann sideways, with kind of a defensive cant to his shoulders. "I was going to ask her to go to the dance with me. You know, the spring formal that's next weekend? And...well, I made the mistake of telling some of my friends. And...they were ragging on me, you know, the way guys do, just joking around, teasing me, and—" He let his breath out in an embarrassed hiss. "Well, I guess Sunny heard."

"What did they say?" Ann asked quietly, dreading the answer. She knew only too well how cruel kids could be.

Will drove a hand through his hair, a gesture he'd either learned or inherited from his father. "Oh...you know, jokes about how we'd look together, because I'm so tall, and she's...well...like you." He grinned charmingly, and then—he had his father's coloring—blushed from his collar to the roots of his blond hair. "There was some other stuff—typical guy stuff, they didn't mean anything by it, but I wish she hadn't heard, if you know what I mean. And then one of the guys—" he took a deep breath and blurted

"—geez, I'm sorry, Mrs. Severn, he said something about the rock quarry. You know all the kids go there to park, right? Well, he asked if I was going to take Sunny there. And he . . . said some really dumb things. Just stupid things. . . ." He looked at Ann with mute appeal, and when she didn't say anything, burst out in frustration, "Look, if she'd just stayed around a little bit longer, she'd have seen me deck the guy! And now she won't even talk to me, or let me explain. . . ." He swore, and quickly apologized. "I don't know what to do."

Ann asked with deadly calm, "Will, what day did this happen?"

Oh, Sunny . . . baby, I'm so sorry.

"Uh, last week sometime. I think it must have been Tuesday. Yeah, I'm pretty sure it was Tuesday."

Tuesday. The day Sunny had tried to run away. Oh, honey, why didn't you tell me?

"Thank you for telling me about this, Will," she said calmly, giving his hand a squeeze. "I'll try and talk to her. Don't give up on her, okay?"

She turned around and managed to make it all the way to her car before she started to shake.

"Sunny? Honey, I'd like to talk to you. . . ."

Sunny turned from the sink with her mouth full of toothbrush and paste. "Does it have to be right now, Mom? I'm going to be late for school."

"Last night you said you were too tired." Ann folded her arms across her chest, an unconscious fortification. "This is important, Sunny."

Sunny made a put-upon grimace through the suds, shrugged and went back to brushing, making Ann feel defeated before she'd even started.

Taking a deep breath to shore up her courage, she ventured, "I talked to Will yesterday."

Sunny's face closed up like a slammed door. She became totally engrossed with rinsing her toothbrush and didn't say a word.

"Honey, he told me what happened. About what you heard."

"Oh, *that*." She turned, leaving a toothpaste-smeared towel in a pile on the counter and wearing an expression of elaborate indifference. "Look, I'm already over that, okay? It's no big deal."

"I think we ought to talk about it," Ann said, standing her ground. "I think you should talk to Will."

"Why?" Sunny dragged a brush through her hair, hauled it into a ponytail holder and gave it an experimental swing. "It's *history,* Mom, really. Will and his friends are just so immature. I really can't be bothered...." She turned from the mirror with a bland, closed-mouthed smile. "Well, gotta go. Bye."

Ann stayed where she was, slumped in defeat against the bathroom wall, while Sunny gathered up her lunch and backpack and went out the front door.

Maybe Niall's wrong, she thought as she heard her daughter out by the front steps, saying goodbye to Sarge, talking baby talk to him just like the old Sunny used to do. For some reason, that lifted her spirits. Maybe Niall was wrong, maybe those people were good for Sunny. Maybe the worst of this was over.

"Hey, Sunny, wait up a minute!"

Will! Sunny's heart gave a painful lurch, which she told herself was stupid, because Will Clemson was nothing but an immature jerk and she didn't even like him anymore. She put her head down, shifted her backpack and tried to walk faster.

Not that it did any good; she could hear the slap-slap of his shoes on the sidewalk as he ran to catch up with her. She could feel herself turning bright red as he fell into step beside her, adjusting his stride to hers. She felt so stupid. Everyone *must* be staring at them. What was it those guys had said? They'd look like capital I, little o coming down the street... Ha, ha, very funny.

"I talked to your mom," Will said, only a little bit out of breath. "She tell you?"

Sunny stopped in the middle of the sidewalk to give him a look of withering scorn. *"So what?"*

At least, she thought with a nice little glow of satisfaction, she wasn't the only one who was embarrassed. Will was turning red, too. He ran his hand over his hair, shifted and mumbled, "Listen, about what happened—about what those guys said—"

"Look, forget about it. I don't want to talk about it, okay?" She took off again, walking as fast as she could. It only took him two steps to catch her.

"Look, Sunny, if you'd just give me a chance to explain—"

"What's to explain?" she said with what she hoped was scathing indifference. "If you and your friends want to act like immature jerks, that's your business!"

At least that stopped him for a minute. Then he yelled after her, "Yeah, well I think *you're* the one who's being immature, if you won't even let me talk to you!" When he caught up with her again she could tell he was mad. "You know something, Sunny? We've sort of been friends since we were little kids, and I always used to think you were a really nice girl—really cute, too. I was just waiting for you to grow up a little so I could ask you out, you know? But you know something? I don't think you're ever going to!"

"Yeah?" Sunny shouted back at him. "Well, I don't need friends like you! I have friends—*real* friends—who wouldn't ever make fun of a person for something they can't help!"

Will looked confused for a moment. Then he swore so violently it made Sunny blink. "Dammit, I wasn't talking about your *height!*"

"Neither was I!" Sunny was breathing hard and her voice was beginning to wobble; any minute now she was going to start crying. And if she cried in front of Will Clemson, she was never going to forgive him, never as long as she lived. "Look, all I know is, friends don't *hurt* each other!"

"Sunny, wait, dammit! I never meant—"

But Sunny was running, running as fast as she could. She didn't really think she could outrun the captain of the basketball team, but she meant to give it a good try. Only this time he didn't come after her.

She ran all the way home, sobbing. When she slammed through her own front gate, all she wanted in the world was a pair of arms to hold her, gentle hands to stroke her hair, a soft voice to tell her it was going to be all right. But her mother was still at the bank, working. No one was home, except old Sarge, waiting for her at the foot of the steps like he always did. Thank goodness for Sarge. At least he loved her, and was always there.

"Hello, old Sargie..." She sank to her knees in the soft dirt beside him. "Oh, Sarge—"

But something was wrong. Sarge didn't wag his tail, or lift his head to lick her hand. Sunny felt her body turn icy, icy cold. She stared down through a shimmering blur of tears and slowly put out her hand. "Sarge?" Her voice became a high, childish whimper. "Oh...no. No...."

Sunny buried her face in the shaggy black fur and sobbed the dry, chest-wrenching sobs of utter desolation.

Ann knew the minute she pulled into the driveway that something was wrong. The front gate had been left open. The number one rule of the house, from the time Sunny was a baby and Sarge a pup, had been that the gate must *always* be closed and latched. It had become a habit so ingrained, not only in Sunny and Ann, but in all who knew them, that its violation seemed as shocking as finding a window broken, or a burglar in the house.

Instead of going in the back door as she usually did, Ann got out of the car and went down the driveway to the street and in through the gate. Halfway up the walk, she knew that Sarge was dead.

"Oh, Sarge." Tears stung her eyes and ran down her cheeks. She sat down heavily on the bottom step and reached out for the last time to fondle the broad black head and drooping ears. He'd died peacefully in his sleep, apparently; she was grateful for that. It was the kindest, gentlest way for a dear old friend to go. And she'd been half-expecting it. But still...it hurt. It *hurt*. Oh, how she was going to miss him. And Sunny—

Oh God, *Sunny*.

Ann ran up the steps and into the house, her heart pounding. "Sunny? Sweetheart, where are you? Sunny..."

She wasn't there. There was no sign that she had been there at all.

This time Ann didn't hesitate. She got out the phone book, looked up the number of the Whispering Pines Motel and dialed it with trembling fingers.

It was Ed who answered. "Hi, Ed, this is Ann Severn," she said, and cut him off quickly before he could begin to get social. "Is, um...Mr. Rankin there?"

"Well, golly, Ann, he sure isn't," Ed said in his slow, easygoing way. "I believe he's gone out of town for a couple days, if you'd like to leave a message for him, I'd be glad to see he gets it."

"Thanks, Ed." Gritting her teeth, Ann depressed the disconnect button with her finger and immediately dialed another number, this one from memory.

When Will answered on the third ring, she asked tensely and without polite preliminaries if he'd seen Sunny.

He gave an angry snort. "Yeah, sure. I tried to talk to her, right after school. I guess you could say we had a fight."

"Oh no..."

"Look, I'm sorry." Will's exhalation was audible and exasperated. "All I wanted to do was talk to her. And then...she yelled at me, and I yelled at her, and she took off for home cryin'. I'm ready to give up. I don't know—"

"Will," Ann interrupted, "Sarge died today."

There was a pause, and then, "Ah, geez. I'm sorry."

"Sunny must have come home and found him. She didn't come in the house, so I think she must have left right after that. Do you have any idea where she might have gone? She had to have been pretty upset."

Will's snort was a duplicate of the first one. "Yeah, I have an idea. I'd lay odds she's with those so-called *friends* of hers—those religious nuts."

Ann pondered that for a moment, frowning. "How would she get hold of them? She told me they don't have phones."

Another snort. "Shoot, they always hang around after school. All she'd have to do is go back over there, or over to the fast-food places on Main Street, and she'd be sure to find a few of 'em." He muttered something profane and apologized for it.

"So you think she might have gone home with them?" Ann asked, ignoring the transgression. "Up to the mountains?"

"Well," Will said grumpily, "that's where I'd start looking."

"Do you know where it is?"

"The compound? Well, I know approximately. I heard Dad talking about it. It's up at Twin Lakes, right below the waterfall. You know where those developers were going to build that fancy resort, and then they ran out of money? Right there. There's a road. It's not paved, but it must not be in too bad shape as much as those kids run back and forth."

"Can you take me there?"

"Take you there? You mean now? Tonight?"

"Yes," Ann said between clenched teeth, "I mean now— tonight."

"Hey, are you sure you want to do that?" Will sounded very young and uncertain, suddenly. "Don't you think you should talk to my dad first?"

"No," Ann said firmly. "Sunny is my child, and this is my problem. I'm going to go get her and bring her home.

If you'd rather not come with me, you can just draw me a map. I'll be there in a few minutes.''

"I'm going with you," Will said quietly, sounding an awful lot like his dad.

An hour later, though, he was sounding young and uncertain again. "Mrs. Severn, are you sure you want to do this?" he asked, peering doubtfully through the windshield of Ann's Bronco. The dirt and gravel road had ended at a wide, solid-looking gate in a chain link fence. It was chained and padlocked, and there was no one—and no lighted structure—in sight.

"Yes, I'm very sure," Ann grunted. She was busy rummaging around behind the backseat of the Bronco. When she came up with Mark's twenty-two, Will's eyes got big and horrified.

"What in the hell are you gonna do with *that?*" he squeaked, not bothering to apologize for the swearing.

Ann gave him a grim smile as she checked the chamber and tucked a small box of shells into the pocket of Mark's nylon hunting vest. "My grandpa taught me you never, ever go into the mountains without a gun, plenty of matches and a warm coat." She patted another pocket. "I've got matches...and here's my coat." She threw her big winter coat, the one with the hood and the sheepskin lining, over her arm and opened the door. "So I'm all set. I'll be fine, Will. You just do what I told you, now, you hear me? You take my car home and you tell your dad to send somebody for me first thing tomorrow morning. Somebody's got to come and open this gate sometime, and when they do, I intend to be here. Now, go on. I left Sunny a note, just in case she's not in here after all. If she comes home, I told her to call your mom and dad, but you might just go by my place and check, in case she's stubborn about it. Okay?"

Will grumbled something under his breath about stubbornness, and Sunny not being the only one, and he knew now where she'd got it from. But although he was big enough to pick Ann up and tuck her under his arm, he was too well brought up to argue with a grown-up.

"Well, okay," he finally said, obviously still unhappy about it. "I just hope Dad doesn't skin me alive for leaving you here. You sure you'll be all right?"

Ann laughed. "I've been camping out in the mountains since I was six years old. Now get out of here. *Go on.*"

She slammed the door of the Bronco and gave it a slap. The motor roared, the headlights stabbed through the trees. She stood in the road and watched the red taillights vanish around a bend before she began following the fence, moving uphill away from the lake, toward the sound of the waterfall. She hadn't told Will her whole plan because he'd been worried enough already, but before she settled down to wait for morning, and for someone to come and unlock the main gate, she intended to do a little exploring. She was going to follow that fence as far as she could, just on the off chance there might be another way into that compound.

Which wasn't going to be easy, because there wasn't much light. Either there wasn't a moon, or it hadn't risen yet; she didn't really keep up on such things. What light there was came from the stars, but once her eyes got used to it, it wasn't too bad, especially since she had the fence to keep her from getting off track. She knew she was probably making quite a bit of noise, stumbling along in the dark like that, but she thought the noise of the waterfall would probably drown out most of it. And anyway, who was there to hear? If there was going to be a guard, he'd be down at the gate.

It was slow going. Sometimes she had to scramble blindly over rocks, or feel her way around fallen trees. Sometimes the pine needles were so thick she couldn't get any footing at all—it was like trying to climb uphill on ice. And all the time the noise of falling water kept getting louder. It grew colder; her nose and cheeks felt numb and damp. The air was filled with a fine, misty spray.

She paused to rest finally, leaning against the rough bark of a yellow pine while she caught her breath and took stock of the situation. She'd about decided she'd gone as far as she could, and was going to head back down the hill, when, without any warning at all, something grabbed her roughly from behind. Something hit her arm, numbing it and sending her rifle flying. She heard it go skittering over the rocks nearby. She opened her mouth to scream, but with the arm across her throat, it came out a strangled squawk, and even that was swallowed up in the roar of the water-fall.

Ten

At first Ann fought mindlessly, striking out in wild desperation with any part of her that happened to be free, at anything she could reach. She was gratified to hear a sharp oath, followed by some impressive swearing; if she was going to die, she didn't intend to go easy.

Then inspiration—or instinct—struck her. She suddenly threw her arms up and went limp, the way small children do when they don't want to be picked up, and slid right out of the oversized coat, leaving her startled assailant with his arms full of empty sheepskin. As she scrambled away on her hands and knees she was thinking with grim satisfaction that there were definitely some advantages to being tiny.

But not very many; her victory was brief. Before she could find her footing in the slippery pine needles her assailant landed on her hard, full length, using all his weight to pin her to the ground. Her face slammed painfully into the prickly needles; the wind whooshed from her lungs; she felt her ribs creak. Some more furious swearing blew past her ear.

And then, as she closed her eyes and braced herself for the inevitable, she heard a hoarse, accented whisper say, *"Good God, Ann, what are you trying to do?"*

Niall. She didn't say his name, or anything else, not out loud. She couldn't speak. She lay still, her heart ricocheting around in her chest, each breath she took dragging through her throat like burlap. She felt his body relax slightly, and his forehead come to rest against her hair, but other than that he didn't move either.

Presently, Ann turned her face to one side, spit out a few pine needles and asked in a conversational tone of voice, "When did you figure out it was me?"

"The minute you got out of your car. Damn it, Ann—"

"You *knew?* You *followed* me?" Her body bucked as she began to fight him again. "You scared me! And you *hurt* me, damn you!"

"Hey," Rankin grunted as he subdued her, "you made it impossible for me not to hurt you. I just wanted to stop you without making any noise. And then you started fighting like a goddam wildcat—"

"Of course I fought! I thought someone was trying to kill me!"

"Don't be silly. If someone was serious about killing you, you'd never know what hit you. What in hell are you doing up here, anyway?"

"I'd like to ask you the same question. Why did you follow me?"

"I didn't follow you, I was already here. And for your information, you were about to blunder into their security system, which would have made things rather difficult for me. *Stop struggling.*"

"I can't breathe! If you'll get off of me—"

"Not until I'm sure you've calmed down. You can breathe fine if you'll just relax, you know," Rankin added reasonably. "I've already taken most of my weight off you."

"Oh." She gave an experimental wiggle, making him suddenly all too aware of what he'd been trying not to think about—her nice round bottom pushed into the hollow of his belly, right below his ribs. Desire bloomed in predictable fashion.

"Ann...." He laid his forehead against the back of her head for a moment and tried to concentrate on even breathing and self-control. It didn't help that her hair was soft as silk and smelled like apples. "What are you doing here, stumbling around in the dark with a *rifle?*"

"I was not stumbling!" She sounded miffed. Then her body suddenly heaved beneath him as a new thought struck her; he almost groaned aloud. "Hey, actually I *was* stumbling, because in case you haven't noticed, it's pitch dark. How did you know who I was, and how did you know I had a rifle, huh?" Her tone was accusing. "Can you see in the dark?"

"Actually," Rankin murmured, "I can." He put his face alongside hers so she could feel his goggles. "See? Special glasses."

"That's *cheating!*" She began to squirm again.

"Ann, it's not a contest," Rankin said, laughing at her outrage. "We're on the same side. I think. Will you lie *still,* damn it?"

"I *will,*" she panted, "if you'll just...let me...turn *over.*"

"Uh-uh. I like you this way." He was breathing hard, too. He moved his body subtly, shifting his legs so that they lay more comfortably alongside hers, making her curves fit his hollows, his hard places her soft ones....

"Why?" Her body was still now, her voice breathless.

Because...if I turn you over I will have to kiss you, he thought. And if I kiss you I will have to make love to you right here, on the ground. I may do it anyway.

He rolled off her and stood up, swearing under his breath. "Let's get out of here," he growled, scooping her coat up off the ground and shaking the pine needles out of it, remembering the start it had given him when he'd felt her slide right out of it. He'd dealt with professionals who weren't as slippery!

When he looked at her again she was sitting up, patting at her front.

"Just checking," she muttered when he asked her what she was doing. "To see if I still have my shells and matches."

"Shells and—" Rankin stared at her in disbelief. The night glasses gave her a ghostly, almost ethereal quality that couldn't have been further from the truth. How could he ever have thought this woman *soft?*

Mumbling to himself in wonderment, he took her hand and hauled her to her feet, then bent over and retrieved her rifle and placed it in her hands. "Come on. I have a place close by. Do you think you can follow me in the dark?"

"I think I can manage to 'stumble along,'" she said in a cool voice, so he knew she hadn't entirely forgiven him.

He'd found the shelter on his first trip, not a cave, exactly, but a dry spot under a rocky overhang, uphill and upwind from the base of the falls. From it he could see everyone who came and went from the compound, which was how he'd known of Ann's arrival. At the same time, because it was well-screened by trees and a billowing cloud of spray, there was very little chance of being seen himself. He'd even built himself a small fire.

"Cozy," Ann commented when she saw it. She looked around, taking in his sleeping bag, the backpack leaning against a boulder, the evidence of his evening meal. Then she carefully laid her rifle down next to the pack, settled herself on the ground with her legs crossed Indian-style, and stretched her fingers toward the fire.

"How long have you been staying here?" she asked casually, like a polite houseguest.

"A couple of days," he said. "Since Sunday."

She wouldn't look at him. "You were here last week, too, weren't you?"

"Uh-huh." He took off the night glasses and stowed them away with the rest of his gear, then went to sit on his sleeping bag, across the fire from her. "Sorry I can't offer you a cup of tea," he said, smiling.

She didn't smile back. Instead she lifted her head slowly and looked straight at him, her eyes glowing like the red-hot coals on the edges of the fire. And now he looked away, feeling as if he'd sucked one of those coals into his throat, wishing to God he could erase her face, those eyes, his need of her from his mind. Guilt crawled through his belly, gnawing at him.

"I want to know why you're here," she said.

"Ann . . . I'm sorry—"

Her chin came up, that stubborn, fightin' look she got sometimes. She didn't raise her voice, but Rankin knew from the edge in it that her emotions were as delicately balanced as a cocked pistol. "Tell me, dammit."

He sighed. "Ann, I wish I could tell you, but I can't. I promised."

"You promised Bill, didn't you?" She gave a short, high laugh. "Listen, did you know that I clobbered Sheriff Clemson with a toy shovel when I was three?" Her voice broke, surprising them both. She put a hand over her mouth and was silent for a few moments, rocking herself slightly and staring into the fire. Finally she straightened, took a deep breath and said in a low, trembling voice, "Niall, I don't know what you're doing here. I don't know what secret business you've got with Bill. And I don't care. I'm sick of secrets. This isn't Berlin, and that isn't the Wall, down there, it's just a damn chain link fence, and my little girl is on the other side of it, and I want her back."

A tear made a glistening track down her cheek. Something twisted painfully in Rankin's chest, so painfully that when she made a jerky movement to brush the moisture away, he gave an involuntary start and murmured, "Don't—"

"I want her back," she repeated in a whisper. "And if I have to shoot somebody to get her back, that's what I'm going to do."

Rankin cleared his throat. It felt as if he'd torn it open. He wished he had the right to comfort her, but he didn't, so instead he said with dry humor, "Well, I don't think it will come to *that*."

It had the desired effect. Ann gave an embarrassed little laugh and wiped her eyes. "I'm sorry," she muttered. "It's been kind of a lousy day." Rankin just waited. After a minute or so she gathered herself, took a deep breath, tried to smile and finally said, "Sarge died today—you know, Sunny's dog? She was already upset, and, um...I think it was just the last straw."

And maybe for her mother, too, Rankin thought, watching her struggle to hold back tears, watching the ripples in her throat that meant she had a lump there she couldn't swallow.

He leaned back on his elbows, hiding his own aching need to take her in his arms behind a familiar facade. *The Gray Man.* That's what they'd called him at the agency, though not to his face. And for more than his prematurely silvering hair and trademark immaculate gray suits. His image was one of absolute control...imperturbable calm...quiet efficiency. His emotions were always straight-line; his manner was low-key, somewhat abstract, a little cold, but in a strange way, reassuring. Like the color gray.

"I'm sorry about your dog," he said, studying her through half-closed eyes. "I know Sunny is bound to be upset, but what makes you think she is in the compound?"

"Because that's where her friends are." Her voice broke. "And you were right, you know. I think—right now she thinks they're her only friends."

"If it'll help," Rankin said quietly, "I don't believe Sunny's in any physical danger."

"I just want her back," Ann whispered, hugging herself, staring at the fire. "She's my little girl, and she loved that old dog. I know she's grieving...and she's lonely. I want her back."

Rankin nodded, and got up to get some more wood, mostly because he couldn't stand to watch her anymore. "We'll go tomorrow morning as soon as they open the gate," he said briskly. "Don't worry, we'll get her back. In the meantime, why don't we try to get some sleep? Come on—you take the sleeping bag."

She shook her head like a stubborn child, pulled her knees up to her chest and wrapped her arms around them. She made a ridiculously tiny and vulnerable bundle, huddled there like an orphaned kitten; she awakened protective instincts in Rankin he hadn't even known he possessed. He felt tender and strong. He felt ten feet tall, ready to slay dragons, brandish swords and make all sorts of foolish gestures and declarations. Foolish...because he knew Ann Severn was about as helpless as a baby rattler, and the mood she was in right now, he thought it likely as not she'd bite his hand if he reached out to her.

"Niall, I want to ask you something." The flames bit into the new fuel and flared in her eyes. "No secrets... please."

"All right," he said equably, settling again onto the sleeping bag. "Ask."

"If there isn't any danger in that compound down there, then why are *you* here? Spying on them, running around dressed like some sort of...of *commando.*"

Rankin looked at her, opened his mouth, and closed it again because suddenly he just couldn't think of a good reason to lie to her any longer. "Ah, God," he muttered finally, shaking his head, "old habits die hard. But you're right, Ann, this isn't Berlin. I promised Bill I wouldn't reveal his involvement in this because he could be in deep trouble if it got out. Do you understand? That's the only reason for the secrecy. He wanted me to...spy on the compound, because he was worried about *their* secrecy— the fence, the barbed wire, the padlocks. He wanted to know what they were up to, that they needed such tight security, and legally he can't touch them. So...he asked me to see what I could find out."

Her look was accusing. "You said you were a stranger, just passing through."

"Oh, I am," he said with soft emphasis. "I am."

"Then how did he know?"

"That I could help him?" His laugh was ironic, even sad. "Because of you, Ann. And Sunny. Sheriff Clemson is very protective of you, you know. Because of my...involvement with you, he had me checked out. He found nothing questionable, just some inconsistencies that made him draw his own conclusions. He's quite intelligent." He chuckled ruefully. "In any case, he asked me, and...I had my own reasons for agreeing to his proposal."

"What were they?" She said it bluntly, almost combatively, as if daring him to tell the truth.

And because he wanted to tell her the truth, he didn't answer her right away. It was another of those moments when a cigarette would have helped, giving him a chance to collect his thoughts. "I was tired," he said finally, not looking at her. "I needed a rest, and this seemed like a good place." A log settled into the fire, sending a small shower of sparks into the mist.

I needed you, he thought, but could not say. I needed your warmth and your softness and your strength. I needed your—

"In any case," he said harshly, "it was probably a mistake. I should not have stayed."

She winced and turned her face away, as if he'd slapped her. "Well, did you find what you were looking for?" she asked after a moment, her voice remote.

Her words startled him, reminding him that when he'd left Washington he had been looking for something, and that his last conscious thought before Sunny and her dog had made their unexpected appearance in his headlights had been to acknowledge that he hadn't found it.

How can I know if I've found what I'm looking for when I don't know what it is?

But he knew that wasn't what she was asking, so he answered with a false, stiff smile, "The reason for the security, you mean? Nothing very sinister...no drugs, orgies, or human sacrifices. Just fear. That's the reason people usually put up defenses, you know.''

"Fear?" Ann frowned. "I don't understand."

"Ann, those poor people down there are expecting the world to end. They truly believe that on a specific day, in the very near future, this planet is going to erupt in the Final Battle. Armageddon. The battle between the forces of Good and Evil. War, Pestilence, Famine...what were the Four Horsemen? Anyway, you get the idea. They believe that they are God's chosen people, that they've heeded His warning, prepared themselves and consequently will survive, but they wouldn't be human if they weren't scared out of their wits. I said no drugs—let me qualify that. I did find out that they've laid in a supply of tranquilizers—not enough for mass suicide, which is what Bill was afraid of, just enough to help combat the nightmares."

"Oh God," Ann said, shuddering. "How horrible. Sunny..."

"If it's any consolation, I don't think most of them know the whole story, especially the young ones. The ones on top don't want to frighten them unnecessarily, I guess. Those kids have been trying to 'save' people, but I don't think they really understand what they're supposed to be saving them from. And I don't think they'd try to keep Sunny from leaving, if she wants to go."

"If she wants to go..." Ann stood up and paced to the edge of the firelight, rubbing her arms. After a moment she turned and said brightly, "So. It sounds as if you've finished your job here. You've done what Bill wanted you to do."

"Yes," Rankin said. "I guess I have."

"So I guess you'll be leaving soon."

"Yes."

He saw her throat move, her face struggle for control. She lifted one shoulder, an oddly poignant little shrug. "Of course. There'd be no reason for you to stay."

Rankin didn't say anything. She just stood there look-ing at him, and he looked back at her, tension keening through the firelight between them and building up inside of him like some kind of sonic feedback, until he couldn't stand it anymore. He sucked in a breath and it fought its way out again, dragging words with it. "Ann, I *can't* stay."

"Why not?" She hadn't meant to say it. She'd prom-ised herself she wouldn't, promised herself she'd have more pride, that she'd never, when the time came, beg him to stay. But of course, it wasn't begging, just to ask. "Why can't you stay, just for a little while?"

His face was tense, frustrated, angry, like something looking through bars. The panther caged. "Because it would be *wrong*. Just like it was wrong the other night for me to take you like I did."

Suddenly, blessedly, she was angry again. "I don't recall you taking anything I didn't give. And I didn't ask you for anything but what you promised me. One night, that's all."

"But now," he said softly, "you're asking me to stay."

And just as suddenly as it had come, the anger was gone. Shame washed her, chilly and bitter as a bucket of cold water in the face. It had the same effect on her as a bucket of water, though—it woke her up. Seeing him like he was now, like he'd been the other night—rugged and whiskery, with his dark hair hanging down over his forehead, look-ing like people she'd known all her life—she'd forgotten who he really was. Forgotten the effortless elegance, the sophisticated manners and tastes—he drank *tea*, not cof-fee—and a kind she'd never even heard of besides! She'd forgotten that he was at home in cities she'd only heard about and was probably never going to see—cities like Paris, London, Washington and Berlin. And of course, the women he was used to would be like him—elegant, sophis-ticated, experienced. Definitely not the kind to get tipsy on one glass of wine.

It took all the pride she had to get her chin up. "Only if you wanted to stay," she said with valiant indifference. "If you didn't have anything better to do."

"Ann, for God's sake..."

"Or, if you just wanted somebody to—"

"Ann." His harsh cry cut off the crude word before she could say it. Eyes the turbulent, violent blue of thunderheads bludgeoned her to silence.

Well, she'd ignored the warning tone in his voice and made him good and mad, and she didn't care. She didn't care. She didn't know why she was trembling, either. She didn't know why it hurt so much to look at him, at his furious face and dark, threatening eyes. She didn't know what was happening to her, or to her world, which until a week or so ago had been peaceful and predictable. And Sunny her only problem.

"You don't know what you're talking about," he said, his voice grating against his iron control. "You have no idea what I'd like, or what I *want*. That isn't the issue. What is, is that I should never have let things go so far between us. I shouldn't have let the other night happen."

"So forget it!" Ann blazed back at him. "Forget it—I have!"

"The hell you have," Niall growled, "and neither have I. That's the trouble—I haven't forgotten a thing I said to you, or did. I said things to you I've never said to a living soul, do you think I'd ever forget that? You've gotten under my skin, Ann, I can't deny that. But what I said the other night is still true. I haven't got a heart to give. And you deserve that, at least. You need someone who'll stay here with you, someone who'll love you—"

"I just wish you'd quit telling me what I need! I don't need anyone, do you understand? I got sick to death of people telling me what I needed after Mark died. I'm strong, dammit! I don't need a man to take care of me. I've been getting along just fine on my own, in case you haven't noticed. At least I was until—" Her voice broke. Until you came along.

Embarrassed and furious, she snatched up her coat, stabbed her arms blindly into the sleeves and flipped up the hood. At least, she thought miserably, it was big enough to hide in.

"Where in the hell do you think you're going?"

"I'm leaving," she said with a sniff, though the idea hadn't occurred to her until that second. "I don't think it's a good idea to stay here with you. I don't think I want to. I'll find my own shelter."

It was a monumental bluff; she was honest enough to admit to herself that it was. Probably, if he hadn't been so angry with her, Niall would have known it, too. And called her on it. But he *was* angry.

"Like hell you will," he growled, coming up off the sleeping bag like a springing tiger. And before she'd gone two steps he'd caught her around the waist and picked her up like a sack of groceries.

"You have entirely too much pride, you know that?" he remarked thoughtfully as she kicked and flailed to no effect whatsoever. "And too much coat—" He set her rather abruptly on her feet and held her with one hand while he peeled the coat off with the other. "You're not going to pull *that* one on me again!"

"You're *hurting* me!"

"I'm not either. Don't you know that's the last thing I'd ever want to do? That's just what I'm trying not to do, to hurt you...."

He stood there with both hands resting heavily on her shoulders, just looking at her, shaking his head. For some reason, his anger seemed to have melted away. He smiled, a slow, sad smile that made her hurt inside.

"I don't know what I'm going to do about you," he whispered. "I shouldn't be doing this. I shouldn't even be touching you."

"I wish you wouldn't say that," Ann said testily. "You make me sound like a bad habit you're trying to give up, like hot fudge sundaes, or cigarettes."

He began to laugh, silently, painfully, and pulled her into his arms. She felt his chest expand, felt a curious quiver go through him, deep, deep, inside. "Ah...damn. You are a bad habit. Well, maybe not a bad one, but I am trying to give you up. I have to. I just...don't want to hurt you."

"How will you hurt me?" she whispered wonderingly. Nothing could ever hurt her again, she thought, if only she could stay right where she was, with Niall's arms around her, his tortured hands cradling her head, shutting out the world.

But of course she couldn't stay there. He wouldn't let her. He pulled away from her a little, tipped her chin up with his fingers so he could look at her and studied her face as if he wanted to memorize it. His eyes were a soft blue now, like a summer sky after the storm has passed. No feelings? No emotions? Just looking at his face made Ann's throat swell and tighten, and a terrible ache spread through every part of her.

"When I go," he whispered, holding her face between his hands like a flower, avidly tracing every line and feature with his rough fingertips. "Or maybe...maybe it's me I don't want to hurt. Because it's going to hurt me to leave you, little one. I don't think I knew until this moment how much."

His hand framed her face while his eyes devoured it like a starving beggar denied entry to the banquet hall, his thumb brushing back and forth across her lips, his fingertips stroking wisps of hair back from her temples. Ann had never known such tenderness, hadn't thought she could hurt so much with tenderness...weep with tenderness. A sob shuddered through her. She opened her mouth, needing to say something, anything, just to release the pressure of too much emotion. But he gently laid his thumb across her lips and shook his head.

"Shh...don't cry," he whispered, closing his eyes as if her pain had gripped him, too. "Just listen to me. When I came here I was searching for something. I knew that but I didn't know what it was, then. I'm still not sure I do, but I think I've found it. The only trouble is—" His laugh was bitter, heart-wrenching. "The only trouble is, I can't keep it. I can't keep *you*. I have to let you go. No, listen to me. You're a settler. You said so, remember? You belong here. This is your world. I don't know what I am. I don't know where I belong. I've spent my life in one kind of world, a world so far from anything you can imagine...or that I could ever make you understand. But that world is changing, or I am. I know I don't belong there anymore, but I don't know whether there's a place for me anywhere else. Right now my world is in limbo. That's what they call purgatory, Ann, and believe me, now I understand why. I can't ask you to share that with me. I can't. *I won't.*"

The last was a fierce and anguished whisper. In its tense aftermath Ann just looked at Niall for a while without moving, though her eyes and nose were humiliating her. Then she shook her head, closed her eyes and sighed in utter exasperation, "God, I *hate* it when you're noble. I'm a grown woman. Don't I get any say in this?"

He shook his head and said in a flat, gentle voice, "No, none at all."

Fear shot through her then like a bolt of cold lightning, all the fear she hadn't felt when he'd talked so casually of killing, or when she'd found his knife in his bed, even when she'd thought she was fighting him for her life. It was fear that sickened her stomach and weakened her knees. Because she knew with absolute certainty that he was capable of taking something precious and irreplaceable away from her, and the irony was, until that moment she hadn't even known how precious it was. Beyond any shadow of a doubt, she knew that he was strong-willed enough, stubborn and implacable enough, *noble* enough to take himself out of her life forever, and to see to it that she never, ever found him if she tried to follow. He could do it. And she thought suddenly that if he did, she wouldn't be able to bear it.

"But what if—" She stopped to clear her throat, trying to keep her voice, at least, under control. "What if I love you?"

She felt him shaking again with that silent, painful laughter. "Ann . . . you can't love me. You've only known me a week."

"What's that got to do with anything?" Self-control, she decided, was vastly underrated. Anger was much better. It hurt less. Trembling with it, she spoke rapidly at first. "Look, I fell in love with Mark Severn when I was ten. He was the only boy I ever dated. We were a couple. It was a foregone conclusion that we'd get married someday. It seemed etched in stone, somehow, even though I knew when he came back from Vietnam that he wasn't the same person I'd fallen in love with. I tried so hard to make it work, but in the end he left me. He *left* me. For years after he killed himself I thought I'd fall in love again. I thought I'd find someone, give Sunny a father, make us a family again. But it didn't happen. I guess I thought it wasn't meant to. And that was okay, because we were happy. *I* was happy. I really didn't need anybody. I *didn't*. Oh, damn you, why did you have to come along?''

She was sobbing now, really sobbing; she doubled up her fists and pounded with supreme futility on Niall's broad chest, knowing her sobs would hurt him much, much more.

"I never needed anybody before, but now I need *you*. How do you explain that? If I don't love you, then how come I feel so lousy, huh? Tell me that!''

"All right—all right!'' He corraled both her wrists in one hand and held them against his chest, right where she could feel the runaway beat of his heart. "Maybe you do love me. I'm hardly an authority on the subject. And that's the point, Ann—*I can't love you back*. I can't. I don't know how. Maybe I did once, but the Niall Rankin who knew how to love died in an East German prison, and I don't...know...how...to get him *back*.'' His hand was tangled in her hair, his fingers tightening unconsciously with each anguished word.

"But you said...you didn't know how to trust, either.'' Ann's voice was hushed, barely audible. "And yet you trusted me. You *did*,'' she said when he just stared at her. "You told me about Marta...and other things. You trusted me. Maybe you could learn—'' she stopped to take a quick, desperate sip of air ''—to love me.''

Eleven

"Love you?" His fingers relaxed, combed through her hair, stroked it back from her face, tenderly traced her hairline, the sensitive shell of her ear. His own face was a study in wonder and frustration. "Ann, I don't even know what to do with you. I don't know if I have anything to give you. I've never known anyone like you before."

"Maybe..." She was lost in the sensation of his hands on her face, in her hair, terrified of what they made her feel... a longing so intense she thought she'd die if he ever stopped touching her. Swamped by the enormity of her emotions, the depths of her vulnerability, her self-esteem foundered and went under. She closed her eyes and whispered miserably, "Maybe what you're really saying is that I don't have anything to offer *you*. I know I'm nothing special. I'm not beautiful, or sophisticated, or anything. I've never been anywhere except L.A., and I don't even know how to drink wine. I don't know why you should—"

She stopped with a small shocked gasp, because his hands—both of them—were tangled up in her hair again.

And because from the way he was looking at her, she could have sworn he was angry again, though what she'd done to make him so she couldn't imagine.

"Nothing special? Nothing to give me?" he rasped. "My God, you sure know how to drive a man crazy, do you know that?"

He stared at her a while longer as the battle raged within him, a battle she knew would cost him dearly no matter what the outcome. She waited in stopped-heart suspense, and when he took her mouth at last, felt a tremendous surge inside, a surge of triumph and newborn self-confidence. As wretched as she'd felt only a moment ago, now she felt new as spring, ancient as earth...invincible...*feminine*.

As hard-fought as Niall's inner battle had been, his surrender was unconditional. She knew that from the way he took her mouth, less a kiss than a claiming—not a caress, but a branding. She knew he wasn't going to hold anything back this time. For now, at least, he'd kicked all the obstacles aside—the guilt, the principles, the reservation of trust and, though he didn't know it yet himself, of love as well. He was going to give it all to her. The thought should have frightened her, but it didn't. Never for a moment did she doubt that she was strong enough, woman enough to match him, passion for passion, gift for gift.

His teeth took tiny bites of her lips, making them burn and tingle. "Nothing...to give me?" he growled against her mouth. His teeth nipped her earlobe. His hot breath and hoarse words sent shock waves along her auditory nerves. "Don't ever say that again."

His teeth raked her throat while his hands held her head prisoner, turning it from side to side to allow his mouth access to her most vulnerable and sensitive places. His tongue probed the indentation at the base of her throat, skated along the edge of her collar until, impatient with that restriction, he pushed it roughly aside and, as if to validate the invasion, lowered his mouth hungrily over the taut, exposed column of her neck. She felt a searing heat, the kind that went clear through her...drawing pressure that pulled at her deepest part. She gave a high, startled cry when her knees buckled.

It was his turn for triumph, the masculine kind. He chuckled, an earthy sound, free of care and full of promise, scooped her up in his arms and, before she had time to worry about the unexpected loss of control, set her down on his sleeping bag.

"Nothing to give me?" The light in his eyes was wild and dangerous. "You have more to give than you could possibly imagine.... You say you need me? I need you like I need air to breathe. I need your softness, your strength, your warmth. Give me your warmth, little one. I've been cold too long...."

She'd have given him her air to breathe, if he'd asked it. The need to give to him was like a deep void, a vast craving, an insatiable hunger. Stunned by the need, she could only stare at him, mute and helpless, not knowing how to fill it.

"Are you cold?" he asked her, smiling at the irony.

She shook her head, only then realizing that she was shivering violently.

"Then come to me...warm me. Let me show you how much you have to give." He unzipped her vest and eased it over her shoulders, smiling when it hit the ground with a thud. "Help me," he whispered as he unbuttoned her shirt. "You'll be warmer that way."

"But you're wearing a sweater," she said peevishly, her voice a jerky, unreliable murmur. "You haven't any buttons."

His chuckle held both tenderness and arrogance. "Oh yes...I do. And if you don't start undoing them soon, I'm going to burst them."

"Oh." She gave a little gulp of laughter and reached for his belt buckle.

But her fingers were so small, weak...useless. His were big, warm...strong. How effortlessly they drew apart the halves of her shirt, pulled them free of her jeans, skimmed her sides and fanned across her back while his thumbs defined the undercurve of her breasts, unerringly found her nipples and stroked them to pearly hardness through the fabric of her bra. She felt like a wand in his hands... slender, yet supple and strong. She swayed toward him, arching her back.

"The buttons, Ann...the buttons." He bent to kiss her, swirling his tongue across her lips and into her mouth, mating briefly with hers and then withdrawing.

"I *can't*," she cried in desperation, "not if you keep doing that!" But somehow she did, and groaned softly with relief and pleasure when she could finally slip her hands inside the waistband of his trousers, ease them slowly down over his hips, feel the silky warmth of his skin, the wonderful, sensual pleasure of hair....

His groan was less soft, and much more carnal. "Ah...God, you feel so good." He had her jeans unfastened, now, too, and was following her lead, molding her hips, cupping her bottom in his hands. He had to bow his back to bring his lips close to her ear when he asked again, "Are you sure you're not cold?"

She shook her head, fascinated by the way his masculine buttocks hardened in her hands.

"Because," he whispered, "I want you naked. I want to see the firelight on your skin."

Her voice seemed wrapped in cotton. She licked her lips and nodded. "Me too."

She should have been cold; in April in the Sierras the night temperatures fell well below freezing. Maybe the air *was* cold, and she was just too full of her own inner fires to feel it. In any case, it felt warm to her, there in the shelter Niall had made, with the curtain of mist and a dark canopy of trees and stars. It was its own world, their world, a primeval world where nothing existed, nothing mattered except the wonder of each discovery. They were like children, and everything seemed new.

When they were both naked, Rankin threw more wood on the fire and came to kneel on the sleeping bag, where Ann already lay in a sensual daze, languorous as a cat. Sit-

ting on his heels, he lifted her hips onto his thighs and drew
her legs around him, so that she lay open to him, and to the
explorations of his hungry eyes and greedy hands.

He caressed her legs, her inner thighs, teased her with
feathering strokes, brushing the rough tips of his fingers
over her silken, satiny places, while she writhed in sensuous abandon and her skin turned moist and dusky in the
firelight. Spanning her waist with his hands, he reached
under her and lifted her so that he could bring her breasts
to his mouth. The nipples were already hard-tipped, the
areolas pink and eager as rosebuds. He nipped them, oh,
so gently with his teeth. She gripped his arms, dug her fingers into his muscles and gasped. Laughing with the sheer
pleasure of her, he nursed her nipples to melting softness in
the heat of his mouth. She moaned. Her head dropped
back and her hair fell, cool and soft as watered silk, across
the backs of his hands.

He laid her down again and slid his hands down the
length of her body, molding her waist, her hips…stroking
her legs, which had begun, now, to tremble. Caressing,
holding her inner thighs. "You're so soft here, did you
know that? Like velvet." His words were like velvet, prais-
ing her. "So warm. Give me your warmth, little one." His
words encouraged her, soothed and enticed her. "Yes," he
murmured as he raised her to him, "give it all to me
now…."

He tasted her honey warmth delicately, his tongue
touching her petals with butterfly strokes, his breath and
passionate whispers melting away the last of her shyness.
Her belly sucked in, her rib cage lifted, her breaths came
sharp and quick and shallow.

But he needed her warmth, hungered for it. And finally
sank into it, finding the center of her warmth and wom-
anhood and losing himself there. He pleasured himself and
her with long, gliding strokes and teasing nibbles, holding
her when she writhed, comforting her when she whim-
pered. He felt the throbbing, the heating, the swelling,
every shaft of pleasurable agony that pierced her. And

when she thought she couldn't take any more, he gave her more...and still more...until with the final deep and tender penetration he wrung from her a cry of such overwhelming joy, and love, and giving, a cry so utterly feminine, and yet wholly *his*....

"*Niall....*"

His name. Just his name, that was all. And it nearly stopped his heart.

Shaken to his core, he gathered her close and rocked her while her body shook with sobs and spasms, stroked her hair while her tears dampened his chest, murmuring words of contrition and comfort. When she finally quieted he said in a broken, wondering voice, "And you thought you hadn't anything to give me."

She nuzzled his shoulder, sniffed and whispered, "But I didn't. You gave to *me*."

"It's the same thing," he said, holding her as tightly as he dared. "Don't you know that?"

She was silent for such a long time that he wondered if, incredibly, she'd gone to sleep like that, sitting astride his thighs. But she finally stirred, raised her head, pulled back and looked right into his eyes. "How come," she said, her face and voice still tear-washed and soggy, "for someone who doesn't know how to love, how come you know so much about it?"

His chuckle had gravel in it. "I know about *loving*, not love. And that's *not* the same thing."

She gazed at him through spiky-wet lashes, plainly not convinced. Then she said huskily, "Okay, teach me. I want to learn how to do to you what you just did to me."

"Somehow I don't think—" The words stopped along with his breath as he felt her mouth on the pulse-spot on the side of his neck. "I don't think you're going to need any teaching." He found her chin and lifted her face back to him. "But later's fine." He kissed her briefly but tenderly. "Rest a while first."

"Uh-uh." She licked her lips, intrigued by the taste of her mingled with the taste of him. "I'm selfish. I want you to give yourself to me the way I did to you.'' She shifted, pinning his hot flesh between her body and his, and began to move sinuously against him. Her smile was sleepy, feline and wholly feminine. "I want you to give me all of you. Now...."

He groaned and grasped her hips, more than ready to oblige; but for the second time that night she surprised him by slithering downward, right out of his grasp. Her throaty little chuckle drifted back to him as her hands encircled him...and then her mouth.

"Ann..." he whispered, and then was silent.

Nothing in his lifetime had prepared him for her. She was wanton as wind, generous as rain, and as curious and uninhibited as a kitten. But more than all those things, what had him feeling stunned and humbled, even as he was trying to keep from exploding, was the *joy* she seemed to find in him. He'd never known a woman to take such pleasure in pleasuring *him*. Because of that, because she was having so much fun, he tried to make it last as long as he could, tried to make it an exercise of will to see how long he could postpone the inevitable. But of course, his willpower had left a lot to be desired, lately.... All too soon he had to grasp her shoulders and haul her roughly up and astride him again.

"I want to be inside you," he growled hoarsely against her mouth, silencing her protests. "Can you stand to have me inside you now?''

For her answer she took his face between her hands, raised herself up on her knees and kissed him, slipping her tongue between his lips and pushing deep, deeper into his mouth as she lowered herself over him...slowly and with excruciating care enfolding him.

The sound that tore through his chest and throat was more than passion. It was altogether a recognition of, protest against, and surrender to a need much greater than the temporary assuaging of hunger or thirst, or sexual desire. It was an acknowledgment of his own loneliness, and of all that he'd forsaken... and a plea for something he knew he couldn't have.

He raised himself and Ann with him, roughly pulled her legs around his waist and her hips hard against him, and drove into her with such violence that her breath rushed from her in a gasp of pure shock. His body shuddered as he withdrew, shuddered again as he buried himself even more deeply in her. Shuddered again... and again. Every muscle in his body clenched and trembled as the cataclysm ripped through him and then gradually subsided, leaving him torn, shaken, and utterly spent.

When the savage darkness lifted, Rankin's first thought was that he'd hurt her. He must have. He'd never been so heedless, so brutal. He was lying full-length, more on top of her than not. Her heart was beating like a trip-hammer against his chest, and he could taste the salt-moisture of someone's tears...someone's sweat...his or hers, it didn't matter. Filled with remorse, he eased his weight off her, kissed her temple and croaked, "Ann, are you...?" He couldn't bring himself to ask.

In a completely normal voice she said, "You don't have to worry about squashing me, you know. I won't break."

He burst out laughing, a release almost as sweet as the one he'd just experienced. He felt warm...light...and for a few moments, at least, completely *happy*. "We'll see about that," he murmured, rolling her into an enveloping hug, "when I have something under you softer than the ground."

She went still for a moment, then said lightly, "Is that a promise?"

The warmth, the lightness, the happiness left him. He kissed the top of her head, then tucked it under his chin and stared up into the canopy of trees and misty, starry sky. "No," he whispered, "no promises." She lay quiet on his chest while he stroked her hair, her arm, her back. "I have one to ask of you, though.... The other night you asked me for one night. Now I want to ask the same of you. Give me tonight, Ann. Don't think about tomorrow, or whatever comes after that. Just . . . promise me tonight.''

"I will," she said in a breaking voice. "I promise."

Later, when she thought he was sleeping, he heard her whisper, "I do love you . . . and you love me, too, Niall Rankin. You don't know it, but I do. You love me. . . .''

He knew, from the terrible ache inside him, that she was right. And that it didn't change anything.

"Someone's coming," Niall said. He slid down from the rocks at the shelter's entrance, puffing vapor into the frosty air.

"From which direction?" Ann asked, turning from the fire, shivering with more than cold. They'd been betting each other who'd get there first, someone from the compound, or one of Bill's deputies.

"Down below. But it isn't Bill, it's your Bronco. It looks like the boy who brought you here."

"That's Will Clemson—Bill's boy." She looked up from struggling into her coat to smile at him, catching in a sharp sip of pine-spicy air at the sight. Niall seemed bigger in the daylight, somehow—bigger, wilder, and more a stranger, in his turtleneck sweater and trousers that weren't jeans, his black beard and brooding eyes. She clung to the memories of the night and added breathlessly, "He's a good kid. And I think he really cares about Sunny."

Niall only nodded; his face was grim and distracted, all business, now. "Okay—ready to go? Come on, you're not taking that thing," he scolded when she reached for her twenty-two, dropping a quick, almost absent-minded kiss on her mouth as he plucked it from her hands. "What do you think this is, a—what do you call it—a posse?"

"I'm taking it," Ann said, the effects of her outthrust chin spoiled somewhat by her chattering teeth. "Look, it's not even loaded."

"Stubborn." Niall's voice softened as he looked at her. He laughed as he caught her in a hug, held her for a moment or two and then let her go. "It's going to be all right," he said roughly. "You're going to be fine. You're going to get her back."

"I know that," Ann said. "I'm okay," Don't think about tomorrow, or anything that comes after....

They found Will pacing up and down in the road, swinging his arms to keep warm and puffing out clouds of vapor. He came running when he saw them, looking red-nosed and worried, but not too surprised to see Niall. He acknowledged Ann's introduction and shook hands without blinking, so apparently Bill had let him in on at least part of the story.

"I'm comin' with you," Will said, glancing at Niall as if he was prepared to argue the issue. "Dad said I could."

Niall just raised one eyebrow and said dryly, "Fine. Now all we have to do is wait for someone to open the gate."

Ann, looking from one to the other, felt dwarfed. "This is ridiculous," she said, huffy with nervousness and maternal anxiety. "I'm not waiting any longer. Look, the two of you could boost me over the fence...."

Will's jaw dropped. He glanced in consternation at Niall, who had a hand over the lower part of his face.

"I don't think that's going to be necessary," Niall said. For some reason he sounded strangled. "I think I hear a car."

Ann glared suspiciously at him, but a moment later forgot everything as the car—a twenty-year-old sedan—came into view through the trees. It stopped in front of the gate and a man with thinning though neatly trimmed dark hair got out, carrying a ring of keys.

"Good morning," he said, smiling beneficently at them. "You must be Sunny's family. We've been expecting you."

Twelve

<hr />

Sunny lay on her side on the narrow cot and listened to the sounds of morning. In spite of the fact that it was warm in the cabin—one of the others must have built a fire in the Franklin stove before leaving—and that she had all her clothes on under the scratchy woolen blankets, she was shivering.

Yesterday... Yesterday and last night had to have been the worst day and night of her entire life.

A tear trickled across the bridge of her nose and dripped onto the pillow; she scrunched her eyes shut and a flood of others followed. So what? It was all right to cry now—everyone was gone. She *hated* to have strangers see her cry.

She didn't know where everyone had gone—to breakfast, she supposed, or prayers. Or to do their chores. Everybody here had some kind of job. She supposed they'd give her one, too....

She'd never felt so lonely. She missed her own bed, her own room, fixing herself a bowl of cold cereal or a peanut butter sandwich whenever she wanted. She missed the bathroom across the hall with all her makeup and stuff in it. She missed Sarge. All she wanted to do was go home and have Sarge be there waiting for her on the front walk, wagging his tail, ducking his shaggy old head, so glad to see her. *Oh, Sarge.*

They'd probably take her home if she asked them. But she didn't want to ask them. She'd feel so stupid, like a homesick little kid. A crybaby.

If only somebody would come. Her mother! Maybe her mother would come and get her.

But her mother didn't know where she was. Sunny hadn't left her a note. And she couldn't call and ask her mother to come and get her, because there weren't any telephones. So forget it. Nobody was going to come.

Oh please, God, let somebody come.

She was so homesick and lonely. She wanted to go home. She wanted her mother. And nobody was going to come.

"Go away," she croaked when she heard the knock. "I'm not up yet."

"Sunny," a kind, cheerful voice called through the door, "someone's here to see you. Will you come up to the lodge?"

Someone to see her? Sunny sat up, her heart pounding. "Just a minute," she called, frantically scrubbing at her face and fumbling for her tennis shoes. Who in the world could it be? She scrambled to open the door, smoothing down her hair and tugging at her sweater. Oh, God, she probably looked terrible!

"Good morning!" It was one of the older women, with a plump round face and grayish-blond hair pulled back in a bun. She was smiling.

"Hi," Sunny said, panting a little as she bent over to tie her shoes. "Who is it, do you know?"

The woman just smiled and held out her hand. "Come," she said, as if Sunny were a little kid, "I'll take you up to the lodge."

Who could it be? Who could it be? Sunny kept thinking as she followed the woman up the steep dirt pathway

through the pine trees to the lodge, which was supposed to
have been a hotel, they said, before somebody ran out of
money. It couldn't be her mother. Her mother didn't know
she was here. *Who could it be?*

The first person she saw when she walked into the lodge
was Niall Rankin; it was hard to miss him, he was so big
and tall. Her heart gave a funny little bump. All sorts of
confused feelings started rolling around inside her, but before she could sort them out, she saw someone else. Someone who was almost as tall as Mr. Rankin, but a lot
skinnier. *Will!* What was he doing here? Oh God, she
thought, if he sees me looking like this, I am going to just
die! She was never going to forgive him for this, as long as
she lived.

The third person in the room was short and roly-poly,
and wearing a huge, bluish-gray coat with a hood. The coat
looked sort of familiar; it made the person wearing it look
just like a giant baby penguin.

And then the penguin turned around.

"*Mom?*" Sunny said in a high, squeaky voice.

The penguin was holding a rifle. Her *mother* had a rifle—a gun! Sunny couldn't believe it. Her mother . . . who
didn't even *believe* in guns, who absolutely *hated* guns, who
thought all guns should be outlawed . . . her mother had a
gun.

Sunny looked at Niall—she wasn't going to look at Will,
not for anything!—then at her mother and back at Niall
again. He just stood there, looking at her in that way he
had, as if he could see right through her. She closed her
mouth, cleared her throat and said with what she hoped
was supreme indifference, "Oh . . . hi, Mom. What are you
doing here?"

"Sunny," her mother said, "I've come to take you home.
Get your things." Her voice was as quiet as always, but
something seemed odd about it.

Sunny folded her arms across her chest and lifted her
chin. "And what if I'd rather stay here?" Maybe it was
pure bravado, just because she hated being ordered around

more than anything, and because Will was standing there, and Niall, and her pride was at stake. And maybe she didn't know *why* she said it. Sometimes she didn't understand herself at all. Like what she said next.

"What are you going to do about it, Mom—shoot me?"

It was a really dumb thing to say. A rotten thing to say. She didn't mean it, but then, she didn't mean half the things she said, sometimes. She looked at Niall again, but he just looked back at her and didn't say a word. Out of the corner of her eye she could see Will sort of shift his feet, like he was embarrassed. For her.

And then her mother shoved the rifle at Niall and came walking toward her. Fast. The hood fell back. And Sunny got the biggest shock of her entire life. Her mother was angry. Her mother was crying. *Crying.* She'd never seen her mother cry, never. Mothers weren't supposed to cry!

Sunny's world spun and tilted. She stood there, stunned, and felt her mother's hands take hold of her arms and shake her, as if she were a little tiny kid. Tears were running down her mother's cheeks, and her eyes were blazing, blistering mad.

"You...will...not...talk to me...like...that!" her mother sobbed as she shook her back and forth. "I am your mother, and I love you, and I have been out... of...my...*mind* worrying about you, do you understand?" Sunny's head bobbed up and down. Her mother shook her some more. "You...are...my...child. My little girl. If anything happened to you, I don't know what I'd do. Don't you *dare* do this to me again, do you hear me? *Do* you?"

Sunny's head bobbed again. She squeaked. "Yes...I'm sorry—"

But her mother wasn't through yet. "And...if... you...*ever* run away from home again, I swear, I'll...I'll break your neck!"

Sunny burst out laughing, then burst into tears. For the first time in a long, long time she felt her mother's arms around her, felt her mother's hands stroking her hair, heard her mother's voice murmur soft, soothing words. For a while she forgot about Niall and Will being there, and when she did remember, she decided she didn't care after all if they saw her cry.

Still, when she finally did stop crying and was mopping up her face and looking for something to blow her nose with, and discovered that Niall and Will had gone outside and left her and her mother alone together, it gave her a strange, warm feeling. She thought it was very nice of them. Thoughtful. Even...sweet.

They were walking down the trail to where the Bronco was parked, Ann and Sunny walking together, Niall and Will behind them. After all that crying, Sunny was feeling very calm and mature. In that kind of voice, carefully watching the ground ahead of her for ruts and pinecones, she said, "Mom, where's Sarge? What did you do with him?"

Her mother just looked at her, kind of at a loss. And then Will blurted out, "I buried him." He moved up to walk beside Sunny, so her mother dropped back to walk with Niall.

"Last night," Will said, lowering his voice so it was just for her, and him. "Out back, you know, by the side of the garage? I made a marker for him, too, but I didn't know what you wanted to put on it. So I thought I should wait until you...well, until you got home."

Sunny looked up at him—way up. And decided she didn't mind that he was so tall, not as much as she used to. "Thanks," she mumbled, and looked back down at the path. Will's hand was very close to hers. She could feel it there. Just as an experiment, she wiggled her fingers...and felt Will's fingers touch the back of her hand. Her hand seemed to want to crawl right into Will's, so she let it. His hand felt warm...good. The way he wrapped his hand around hers, like it was something precious he wanted to take care of, made her feel like that all over.

She didn't want to turn around to look, but she wondered.... She wondered if Niall Rankin was holding her mother's hand, and whether it made her mother feel the same way as she did when Will touched her. She wondered....

"About the dance," Will said, loudly clearing his throat. "You still... I'd still like to go with you. If you..."

"Okay," said Sunny. For a moment she thought she might cry again, but then she looked up at Will and smiled instead.

"I looked for you at the bank," Niall said. "They told me that you were sick. Are you all right?"

"I'm fine." Ann smiled and pulled the door wide, stepping back to let him in. The back door was open, too, so the warm afternoon wind came with him, smelling of earth and lilacs, sage and pine, and a touch of diesel fuel. The familiar smells of Pinetree.

"I just felt...after this morning...last night...I couldn't go to work. I needed some time—" She stopped and drew an uneven breath. "Sunny and I have a lot of talking to do. A lot to work out."

"I know," Niall said softly. "I know." He stood there, looking around him, reminding Ann of that first night when it had seemed to her as if he'd never seen such a place before. As if he'd just dropped in from another world. As, in a way, he had.

"So," she said. "You're back from the mountain, then?" It was one of those silly questions people ask when they don't know what else to say, the answer to which is already obvious. He was showered and clean-shaven, dressed in his elegant, immaculate clothes, looking as he had that first night—sophisticated, aloof, foreign. The man she'd held through the night on the mountain, the man whose face and body were already as familiar to her as her own and far more precious, seemed only a memory.

"You've finished your business with Bill?"

"Yes. I've given him the film and my analysis of the situation. He seems reassured." He frowned at her, jingling keys in his pockets.

The answer to her next question was also obvious. She couldn't bring herself to ask it.

"Ann, I—"

There were voices, a clattering of footsteps in the kitchen. Sunny and Will came in, taking up more than their share of space, the way teenagers always seem to. Will had some boards under his arms, and Sunny was carrying an assortment of tools. Will said something polite and shook hands with Niall, then went on into Sunny's bedroom.

Sunny folded her arms across her chest, stuck her chin in the air and said briskly, "So—you're leaving." It was the old Sunny, the smart-mouthed, chip-on-the-shoulder Sunny, but Ann didn't shush or scold her.

"Yes," Niall said quietly. "I'm afraid I have to."

Sunny's mouth twisted in a bitter little smile. "Yeah, it figures. I knew you would." She shrugged, all bright and nonchalant again. "So—where you goin'? L.A.?"

"Yes," Niall said, "I have to see a man there. I promised I would."

"You coming back?" The question was oh so casual, but there was a defensive cant to Sunny's shoulders. Ann held her breath.

After a long pause Niall said, "I don't know. Maybe I will."

"You won't," Sunny said flatly. She turned, walked into her room and shut the door.

Niall looked at the closed door for a moment, then looked at Ann and arched an eyebrow. "Should they be in there together like that? I know I'm not an authority, but it seems to me—"

"They're making a marker for Sarge's grave," Ann explained.

"I know, but—"

Ann had to laugh at the look on Niall's face—a look of almost classic parental consternation and confusion.

"Anyway," she said gently, "I trust Will. His dad would skin him alive if he ever got Sunny in trouble, and he knows it. Besides…" Her smile softened. "I know he cares about her too much to ever do anything to hurt her."

"So," Niall said, drawing in a breath and looking out the window, "I guess… like mother, like daughter."

She didn't have to ask him what he meant. "That's the way it is here," she said with a small shrug. "Growing up together, falling in love, getting married. Sometimes it even lasts… a lifetime."

"Ann, I'm sorry."

"Why did you come?" The question burst from her before she knew. She hadn't wanted to do this—hadn't wanted to cry. Promised herself she wouldn't. She glanced over her shoulder at the closed door to Sunny's room and lowered her voice to an anguished whisper. "How can you do it, Niall? How can you leave? After—"

"After last night, you mean?" His voice was hoarse, guttural, almost bitter. "After having the incredibly poor judgment to fall in love with you? Don't you understand, Ann? That doesn't change things, it only makes it harder. Everything I said to you up there on the mountain still goes."

"Then why did you do this?" It was terrible, trying to whisper through tears. "Why didn't you just let it go at that? Why did you have to come to say good-bye? Don't you know how much it *hurts?*"

"It hurts me too, damn it. Don't think it doesn't." He lifted his hands as if he wanted to touch her, then let them drop. And yes, the longing was there, in his eyes. It was all there—everything that had gone between them in the night. For some reason, it only made Ann's own pain worse. "Why did I come? I came because I wanted to see you once more, I guess. I wanted to hold you… once more. But—" His voice broke; he made a helpless gesture toward Sunny's closed door.

Ann made a tormented sound, half sob, half laughter. "Yeah, I know. That's the way it is when you've got teenagers in the house." She shrugged, too, as full of longing and as helpless as he. All they could do was stand there and look at each other, while the pain vibrated between them like a palpable thing.

"Would you like to go for a walk?" Ann said finally, her voice high and bright with suffering.

Niall just nodded and took her hand.

It was a beautiful spring afternoon, bright with sunshine, busy with the sounds of insects and birds, heavy with the scent of growing things. Too beautiful a day, Ann thought, for so much pain.

They walked in silence until they came to Mrs. Jensen's house, where the lilac bush hung over the fence. Niall stopped and broke off a sprig and held it to his nose, glanced at Ann and smiled... a wry, sad smile.

Make a memory.... She could hear herself say that— could it only have been a week ago? It was frightening, how quickly things could happen. How suddenly things could begin—and end. One minute you thought your life was all set to go in one direction, and then you met someone, just one person, and suddenly nothing was the same... everything was changed.

I can't let him go, she thought in sudden panic. *I can't.*

"Suppose," she said, clearing her throat, since her voice seemed to have rusted, "suppose I went with you."

Niall looked at her, his eyes shadowed and sad. Then he looked down at the flower he held in his battered hand and slowly shook his head. "It wouldn't work," he said, carefully placing the blossom in her hand. "You'd be miserable. You're a settler, remember? You need your roots. Without them you'd wither and die, just as surely as this flower is going to die before night. And what about Sunny? She needs her roots, too. How can you even think of taking her away from the only home she's ever known... away from that boy back there?"

"Sunny's young," Ann said desperately, struggling against the undeniable, like an impaled butterfly. "Who knows, maybe she's a pioneer at heart. Did you know what you wanted when *you* were fifteen?"

"When I was fifteen...." Niall smiled and closed his eyes, shielding the pain in them from her. "Ann, when I was fifteen, I was so idealistic, I don't think I ever gave a thought to what *I* wanted. Before that, all I was concerned about was surviving. I never knew my father. He was an American G.I. who left for home before I was born." He gave a short, mirthless laugh. "All he left me was a name I've had to spend a lifetime explaining. All I remember of my childhood is the constant struggle to find enough food to fill my belly. I worked, I stole, I begged—whatever it took. My mother died when I was twelve—I think it was the struggle that killed her—and after that, believe it or not, it was easier for me. Because then I only had to worry about feeding one person....

"I got involved with the East German underground when I was fifteen—just Sunny's age. From then on, I fed on ideals. For the first time I had a *purpose,* something that elevated me above the level of animals. Do you understand? Helping people to freedom was my reason for being alive, my justification for taking up space on this planet. I never gave a thought to where I belonged, or of having a home and a family some day. Even when I fell for Marta, she was still a part of... of all of that—the danger, the excitement, the purpose. I never thought about what I'd do when the purpose was gone...."

"I think I understand," Ann said slowly, gazing at him through a mist of tears. "You've been involved in it—that cause—in some way all these years, haven't you? And now, all those things we heard about on the news—the Berlin Wall coming down, all of that—it's over. All those years you told me you were such a cold, heartless machine—but you were still just that idealistic boy, weren't you—still fighting for a cause. And now it's over."

She stopped, choking on a sob, and looked down at the gate in front of her—her gate. She put her hand on it, the hand that held the sprig of lilac.

"Niall?" She looked up at him, but he turned his head quickly, not wanting her to see his face. She sniffed and tried to wipe away some of the moisture on her own. "You told me...when you came here you were looking for something, but you didn't know what it was. And then up there...on the mountain...you said you thought you'd found it—meaning me—and that you couldn't keep it. But...did you ever think—maybe I'm not what you were looking for? At least, not all of it."

He was staring at her now, but she could barely see him through the blur of her own tears. "Did you ever think...that maybe what you've been looking for...is just a place to call *home?* A place...to sink your own roots, maybe even have that family you never had. Did you ever think about that?"

Niall didn't say anything. After a tense, held-breath eternity, Ann let a sob go and pushed blindly through the gate. Then she turned back, reached up to take his face in her hands, stood on tiptoe and kissed him. For a moment, an instant, he resisted her. Then his mouth softened, his hands gripped her shoulders, and a low groan issued from deep in his chest.

It hurt to kiss him. Oh, how it hurt. Her face, her throat, her chest... She felt as if she were breaking into tiny pieces. It was torture...pain she didn't think she could survive. But she kissed him a long, slow, aching time, letting him feel her trembling, letting him taste her tears. And then she pulled away.

"Think about that," she whispered. "And if you ever figure out I'm right, well, you know you've got a home here. Right here."

She pushed on through the gate again, ran up the walk, up the steps and into the house. Sunny came out of the bedroom when she heard the front door slam. She took one look at Ann and said roughly, "Well, did he leave?"

"Yes," Ann whispered.

"Do you think he'll come back?"

Ann looked down at the sprig of lilac in her hands. Her hands were wet, and she didn't know if it was her tears, or Niall's. She shook her head. "I don't know."

Sunny came and put her arms around her and held her and patted her back, like a mother comforting a heartbroken child. "It's all right, Mom," she whispered. "We're going to be all right, you'll see."

The day of Armegeddon had come and gone. There'd been a little rain that day—not much, just enough to dampen the poppies on the foothill slopes and melt the last snow at the resort elevations. Tourists were pouring into the Eastern Sierra towns, armed with cameras to photograph the desert wildflower show, which was turning out to be especially beautiful this year. And little by little the residents of the Doomsday Compound, as the local wags had taken to calling it, were beginning to drift away, some to try to pick up the pieces of lives they'd abdicated, a few to go back to the books and prophecies, to see if they could figure out where they'd gone wrong.

All this Rankin learned from Bill Clemson, when he stopped by his office to tell him he'd decided to take him up on his offer to go trout fishing.

"I don't know," Bill sighed, tipping his chair back and stretching so he could see out the window. "It seems kind of sad to me, living every day thinking the world's about to come to an end. I couldn't live that way. Yeah, I know the scientists tell us the world's going to end someday, probably in a few million years or so, when the sun burns up, or we collide with a comet. But that doesn't bother me. I figure there probably won't be any humans around then, anyway. We'll have evolved into something else. Nah...me, I've got to believe there's always going to be another spring, you know? Another chance to start things all over again, fresh and clean and new."

In a way, that about summed up the way he felt, Rankin thought as he went through Ann's front gate—fresh, clean...new.

Sunny was sitting on the steps. She didn't look as if she was there for any particular reason; it was almost as if she'd been waiting for him. She didn't say a word as he strolled toward her, just eyed with distrust the cardboard box he was carrying. The box had a carry handle and holes punched in the sides, and was meant for cats, but the vet had assured Rankin it would do fine for his purposes.

He set the box down near the empty depression in the soft earth beside the bottom step.

Sunny looked at it the way she might a box full of snakes.

"Don't just sit there," Rankin said. "Open it up."

"I hope it's not more wine," Sunny muttered. But she opened the box. And then she didn't say anything. Rankin saw her throat move a couple of times, and then she looked up at him—a hostile, narrow-eyed glare. "What do you call this? A bribe?"

"No," Rankin said blandly, "I call it a puppy."

He scooped it out of the box and set it on the bottom step next to Sunny's feet. The puppy sat for a moment or two getting his bearings, then got up, waddled over and began to chew on Sunny's shoelaces.

She watched him for a minute, then threw her hair back over her shoulder, an "I-don't-give-a-damn" gesture. "What makes you think I need a puppy?"

Rankin lifted an eyebrow. "Nobody *needs* a puppy, any more than they need a snotty teenager." Sunny snorted. "This particular puppy happens to need a home. I thought you might be interested."

"Yeah, right," said Sunny. She jerked her foot, surprising the puppy, who lost his balance and rolled off the step. He gave a wounded yelp as he tumbled like a furry black pill bug onto the walk. With a contrite cry, Sunny scooped him up, cuddled him under her chin and began to soothe his injured feelings with apologies and baby talk.

"I couldn't find one like Sarge," Rankin said conversationally as he watched the puppy bathe Sunny's face with his tongue. "I don't know what kind of breed he was. This one is a shepherd, though, just a different kind."

"Oh yeah? What kind is he?"

"German shepherd," Rankin said, straightfaced.

"He seems awfully hyper," Sunny said, scowling as she removed a strand of hair from the puppy's mouth.

"All puppies are hyper. He's going to need a lot of training. Discipline. You'll probably have to have some help with him."

"Yeah?" Sunny transferred the scowl to Rankin and said rudely, "Who's going to help me? You?"

Rankin shrugged. "Sure. If you want me to."

"You planning to be around?" The question was casual...cautious. "I thought you were just passing through."

"No," Rankin said, "I plan to stay awhile."

"How long?"

Rankin rubbed the back of his neck and said, "Well, I guess that depends on you...and your mother. Long as you want me to."

Sunny considered that. "Where are you planning to live? Here?"

"I thought I might." Rankin said. "That okay with you?"

Sunny rejected that idea flatly. "The house is too small. There's only one bathroom."

Rankin put his head back and looked thoughtfully at the house. "I was thinking about adding a few rooms—a bigger kitchen, maybe a master bedroom, if your mother likes the idea."

Sunny squinted at him; the puppy was content, for the moment, chewing on her knuckles. "Can I have my own bathroom?"

"If you keep it clean." He stuck out his hand. "Agreed?"

Sunny thought it over. "Agreed," she said. She sounded tentative, but gave his hand a shake to seal the deal. "Oh, by the way—just in case you were wondering." Her words were muffled as she buried her face in the puppy's fur. "Mom's in the house."

"Thanks," Rankin said dryly.

But he'd known she was there from the beginning. Watching him from the big front window. His awareness of her was like an electrical charge running through his muscles. His need to see her, to talk to her, hold her, was a keening in his ears, a fire on his skin, a thirst that could drive a man crazy. And he had the worst case of nerves he'd ever had in his life.

She wasn't in the living room. He found her in the kitchen, banging dishes around, and he could tell she'd been crying.

He'd thought about what he'd say to her, what he'd do. He'd practiced speeches. Now he couldn't remember a thing. He'd never felt so unprepared. He went to her, lifted his hands but didn't touch her, and finally said brokenly, "For God's sake, help me, Ann, I'm new at this."

"New at what?" She was shaking; he could hear it in her voice. But then, so was he.

"Love. I told you, I don't know anything about it. I'm okay with the loving, but—" He gave a helpless shrug.

There was a long pause. A sniff. "Then why don't you try the loving," she said, turning to him at last, "and maybe the rest will come to you."

Had he kissed before? He knew he had, a thousand times, a thousand ways...but never, ever like this. This was sweet as lilacs on a springtime evening, warm as brandy before a roaring fire, wicked as tumbled sheets on a Sunday morning. It was someone humming love songs in the kitchen; soaping his back, and all the rest of him, in the shower; sharing a newspaper over tea in the morning; falling asleep with her head on his shoulder. It was Ann. It was coming home.

"Niall...we can't...do this. Not now..." She hauled herself away from him, then swayed back again, seeking his mouth as a thirsty wanderer seeks a cooling spring. "No...we can't," she mumbled against his lips. "Sunny's outside."

"I know. She told me where you were." His hands were under her sweater, greedy for her, hungry...yearning.... "She won't bother us for a while."

"I know...but still...." Her mouth looked swollen, her eyes dazed.

Rankin sucked in air and pulled her close. "I know," he said, letting the breath out in a gust of rueful laughter. "It's what happens when you have teenagers in the house." His hands skimmed up her sides, over her shoulder blades and then withdrew. He patted her sweater into place and sighed as he wrapped her into a hug. "I'll have to make some adjustments."

"Niall," she whispered after a while, pressing her face against his chest, " —you're shaking."

"You bet I'm shaking." His laugh proved it. "I'm terrified." In all the years of living on the edge, of playing the deadly cat-and-mouse games, he'd never been so frightened. "It's the most terrifying thing I've ever done," he said in an awed voice. "This business of loving someone."

She pulled back far enough to look at him, her eyes blazing through tears. "What do you mean, someone? You love *me*, dammit. Say it."

Rankin looked into them and felt for a moment as if he were drowning. "I love you, dammit."

"That's a little better," Ann whispered huskily. "I intend to give you lots of chances to practice it. Practice makes perfect, you know."

He sucked in air and held her so tightly he thought he heard her ribs crack. "That's what scares me. I haven't had any. I still don't know whether I'll be any good at it—loving you. I've been a loner for so long.... I'm a cold, hard man, Ann. My emotions are rusty. What if I disappoint you? When I think about the *responsibility* of loving, the gift of you loving me... When I think about tomorrow, all the tomorrows, and how much you deserve, it scares me. Because I don't know if I can give you as much as you deserve."

"Niall..." Her strong hands touched his face, holding him still, silencing his words. "Don't think about tomorrow, or anything that comes after that. Just promise me today...and tonight. That's all I will ever ask of you. Just today and tonight. Can you give me that much?" Her eyes were shining with warmth and love; love that overflowed as he watched and ran in a glistening track down her cheek.

"Yes," he whispered and closed his eyes, feeling her warmth and love wash over him, taking it in through his pores. "I think I can promise you that much."

"And I promise you the same. And...if we ask each other that same question every morning—give me only today and tonight—what will you answer?"

"Yes," he murmured fervently, as he felt himself fill up with warmth until he overflowed with it too, and his shaking stop and his fear drift away like sparks in the night. "I'll always give you today...and tonight. *I promise.*"

He kissed her while the warm spring wind blew through the back door—fresh, clean...new.

*   *   *   *   *

Silhouette Books ®

Dear Reader,

Over the past few months, a new schedule for on-sale
dates of Silhouette series has been advertised in our
books. These dates, however, only apply to the United
States. We regret any inconvenience or confusion that
may have been caused by this error.

On-sale dates have not changed in Canada, so all your
favorite Silhouette series will be available at your local
bookstore on their usual dates.

Yours sincerely

Silhouette Books

SREADER

MILLION DOLLAR JACKPOT
SWEEPSTAKES RULES & REGULATIONS
NO PURCHASE NECESSARY TO ENTER OR RECEIVE A PRIZE

1. Alternate means of entry: Print your name and address on a 3″×5″ piece of plain paper and send to the appropriate address below.

In the U.S.	In Canada
MILLION DOLLAR JACKPOT	MILLION DOLLAR JACKPOT
P.O. Box 1867	P.O. Box 609
3010 Walden Avenue	Fort Erie, Ontario
Buffalo, NY 14269-1867	L2A 5X3

2. To enter the Sweepstakes and join the Reader Service, affix the Four Free Books and Free Gifts sticker along with both of your other Sweepstakes stickers to the Sweepstakes Entry Form. If you do not wish to take advantage of our Reader Service, but wish to enter the Sweepstakes only, do not affix the Four Free Books and Free Gifts sticker; affix only the Sweepstakes stickers to the Sweepstakes Entry Form. Incomplete and/or inaccurate entries are ineligible for that section or sections of prizes. Torstar Corp. and its affiliates are not responsible for mutilated or unreadable entries or inadvertent printing errors. Mechanically reproduced entries are null and void.

3. Whether you take advantage of this offer or not, on or about April 30, 1992, at the offices of D.L. Blair, Inc., Blair, NE, your sweepstakes numbers will be compared against the list of winning numbers generated at random by the computer. However, prizes will only be awarded to individuals who have entered the Sweepstakes. In the event that all prizes are not claimed, a random drawing will be held from all qualified entries received from March 30, 1990 to March 31, 1992, to award all unclaimed prizes. All cash prizes (Grand to Sixth) will be mailed to winners and are payable by check in U.S. funds. Seventh prize will be shipped to winners via third-class mail. These prizes are in addition to any free, surprise or mystery gifts that might be offered. Versions of this Sweepstakes with different prizes of approximate equal value may appear at retail outlets or in other mailings by Torstar Corp. and its affiliates.

4. PRIZES: (1) *Grand Prize $1,000,000.00 Annuity; (1) First Prize $25,000.00; (1) Second Prize $10,000.00; (5) Third Prize $5,000.00; (10) Fourth Prize $1,000.00; (100) Fifth Prize $250.00; (2,500) Sixth Prize $10.00; (6,000) **Seventh Prize $12.95 ARV.

   *This presentation offers a Grand Prize of a $1,000,000.00 annuity. Winner will receive $33,333.33 a year for 30 years without interest totaling $1,000,000.00.

   **Seventh Prize: A fully illustrated hardcover book, published by Torstar Corp. Approximate Retail Value of the book is $12.95.

   Entrants may cancel the Reader Service at any time without cost or obligation (see details in Center Insert Card).

5. Extra Bonus! This presentation offers an Extra Bonus Prize valued at $33,000.00 to be awarded in a random drawing from all qualified entries received by March 31, 1992. No purchase necessary to enter or receive a prize. To qualify, see instructions in Center Insert Card. Winner will have the choice of any of the merchandise offered or a $33,000.00 check payable in U.S. funds. All other published rules and regulations apply.

6. This Sweepstakes is being conducted under the supervision of D.L. Blair, Inc. By entering the Sweepstakes, each entrant accepts and agrees to be bound by these rules and the decisions of the judges, which shall be final and binding. Odds of winning the random drawing are dependent upon the number of entries received. Taxes, if any, are the sole responsibility of the winners. Prizes are nontransferable. All entries must be received at the address on the detachable Business Reply Card and must be postmarked no later than 12:00 MIDNIGHT on March 31, 1992. The drawing for all unclaimed Sweepstakes prizes and for the Extra Bonus Prize will take place on May 30, 1992, at 12:00 NOON at the offices of D.L. Blair, Inc., Blair, NE.

7. This offer is open to residents of the U.S., United Kingdom, France and Canada, 18 years or older, except employees and immediate family members of Torstar Corp., its affiliates, subsidiaries and all other agencies, entities and persons connected with the use, marketing or conduct of this Sweepstakes. All Federal, State, Provincial, Municipal and local laws apply. Void wherever prohibited or restricted by law. Any litigation within the Province of Quebec respecting the conduct and awarding of a prize in this publicity contest must be submitted to the Régie des Loteries et Courses du Québec.

8. Winners will be notified by mail and may be required to execute an affidavit of eligibility and release, which must be returned within 14 days after notification or an alternate winner may be selected. Canadian winners will be required to correctly answer an arithmetical, skill-testing question administered by mail, which must be returned within a limited time. Winners consent to the use of their name, photograph and/or likeness for advertising and publicity in conjunction with this and similar promotions without additional compensation.

9. For a list of our major prize winners, send a stamped, self-addressed envelope to: MILLION DOLLAR WINNERS LIST, P.O. Box 4510, Blair, NE 68009. Winners Lists will be supplied after the May 30, 1992 drawing date.

Offer limited to one per household.

LTY-S791